YOURS TO CHERISH

LANTERN BAY, BOOK 3

DIANA FRASER

BAY BOOKS

Yours to Cherish
by Diana Fraser

Archaeologist Madeleine MacGillivray arrives in Akaroa, New Zealand, with a backpack and a story she refuses to tell. Mysterious women are a weakness of Dr Gabriel Connelly's—especially if they're beautiful. But, despite an undeniable chemistry, Madeleine insists on remaining friends only.

However, Gabe has six months in which to change her mind; six months in which to unlock the mystery surrounding the lovely, mysterious Madeleine. But, after he discovers the truth, will he wish he hadn't?

—Lantern Bay—
Yours to Give
Yours to Treasure
Yours to Cherish
Yours to Keep

Print Edition
978-1-927323-54-0

For more information about this author, visit:
http://www.dianafraser.net

1

Madeleine MacGillivray watched the departing bus lumber up the hill and over into the next valley, leaving behind a trail of dust. She shifted her rucksack on her shoulder and looked around. The sea was a pale shade of green in the early morning light, reflecting the color of the trees and open hillsides on the opposite side of Akaroa Harbor, the detail obliterated by the brilliant glare of the sun that had just emerged over the farther hills. It was a larger harbor than she'd imagined when he'd told her about it.

To her other side, the town was a mixture of old and new —a two-story colonial building with its rounded metal roof and white pillars and fretwork was freshly painted and still held the prime position overlooking the tree-lined harbor. Around it were ranged newer, single-story buildings which housed shops and cafés, set around paved pedestrian areas, dotted with umbrellas perched over café tables and terra cotta pots filled with fragrant lavender.

So this was it. Akaroa. The place she'd heard so much about. While the harbor and hills were bigger than she'd imagined, the town was smaller. Behind the shops that fringed the shoreline were the houses, some small, some grand, that rose around and above the bay, to the highest ridge. But that was it.

She grunted softly. Just showed how much the place had meant to him. He'd built it up when he'd recalled it, to something far more imposing. She could imagine him growing up here, his big personality dominating the small community, just as he'd been the center of her world. She felt a chill seep into her heart before she stopped it dead. She couldn't think of that now.

She hitched the bag higher onto her shoulder and walked along the footpath. The town was a strange mixture of European charm—with its cute, cottagey veranda-shaded decks and brightly planted hanging baskets—and New Zealand drama. The pale, wheaty-green hills which sheltered Akaroa were the product of seismic activity, and appeared rumpled and creased as if a soft cloth had been pushed together. And the native trees—gnarled and spreading—were like huge, ancient, ungainly giants. Born in Denmark, she was accustomed to European charm and, having worked in the US, terrain shaped by seismic activity wasn't new to her, but the whole picture combined into a landscape which was uniquely New Zealand.

It was still early, but there were already people around. Outside one café a woman was busy typing into a laptop, and a middle-aged man was getting stuck into a cooked breakfast which smelled divine. From across the road an old lady emerged carefully from a building whose front door opened directly onto the street.

As Maddy walked past the building, she noticed it was a doctor's surgery. Below the sign, obscuring the doctor's name, was a handwritten sign saying "Drowning in paperwork—Need help!" Brightly colored flowers decorated the sign.

The old lady laughed when she saw it and called out a name which Maddy couldn't quite hear as she crossed the street. A taxi drew up outside the surgery, obscuring her view. Only the top of a man's head, his golden curling hair bright in the morning sun, was visible to her. It was pretty hair. It was curl-it-around-your-fingers kind of hair. It was hair that tugged a little at her memory. She paused and turned a stand on which picture postcards were displayed. As the picturesque images of Akaroa whirled in her vision, her mind focused on the voice of the man with the curly hair. She couldn't hear what he said, just his deep ironical tone. Whatever his words, it made the old lady laugh even louder. Other voices joined in as passers-by greeted them. They were both obviously well known to the community.

It seemed to take an age before the old lady was safely deposited into the taxi, but Maddy continued to wait. She had a curious desire to see what the rest of that golden-haired man with a deep voice looked like. But, by the time the taxi pulled away from the sidewalk, the door was closed and there was no golden-haired man in sight. And the sign was gone.

She shrugged and moved on.

There were more cafés and shops advertising tours and events aimed at tourists than she'd imagined. But not so many as to spoil its character. Her stomach growled at the smell of fresh baking and she looked around for its source. She hadn't eaten since she'd got off the plane early that morning. She'd come straight to Akaroa—an hour out of Christchurch—on the bus, and was starving.

She peered in the window of a small café. Freshly baked loaves, whose glaze was enriched by the early morning rays of the sun, filled the window. Together with the pastries, they could have graced the most sophisticated French patisserie. Then a woman appeared and slipped a tray into the window, filled with melt-in-your-mouth croissants, the warm chocolate oozing out of the ends. The woman looked up, caught her eye and smiled. Maddy smiled back hesitantly. It didn't pay to catch people's eye in some of the places where she'd traveled, and she'd developed a caution with people which he'd used to tease her about. Now she was here, in his hometown, she understood his amusement. It was the kind of place where trust was more in evidence than suspicion. And the woman in the café was no exception. Her smile hadn't faded, despite Maddy's wariness.

Instinct told her to leave, but he'd insisted she come here if anything ever happened to him, and she'd promised him she would, never in a million years imagining she'd have to keep her promise so soon, if ever. So here she was, forcing herself not to run away at the sight of a warm smile. She swallowed, pulled her bag more securely over her shoulder and walked into the shop.

The old-fashioned doorbell jingled, and Maddy stepped into another world.

"Hi!" the woman called out, as she made her way back behind the counter. "You're new here, aren't you?"

Maddy nodded. "Yes. Arrived this morning."

"Staying long?"

Maddy hesitated, trying to fight the need to leave, to run away from this woman whose interest she really didn't want. "A few months. Or more," she added quietly. She didn't want to go around admitting that she'd committed herself to staying six months in Akaroa. People would ask questions, and that was one of the conditions she'd agreed to. No one must know.

"Ah, I thought you had a different look about you. When I saw you I thought to myself, that's not someone who's just passing through." The woman grabbed a paper bag. "Would you like some of chef's baking? I'd offer you mine, but it's an acquired taste, so I've been told." She grinned disarmingly, once more. "What would you like?"

Maddy looked longingly at the pies, whose flaky pastry lifted at the edges, promising succulent meat within, as she mentally converted the New Zealand dollars to US. She didn't have much money and, until she found a job, she had to be careful. She selected one of the smaller pies. "How much is this?"

The woman watched Maddy open with a click the well-used leather purse where she kept her loose change. "On the house." The woman stretched over and plucked a still-warm chocolate croissant. "Here and take one of these too."

Maddy opened her eyes wide with surprise and then frowned. "It's okay, I can pay."

"I'm sure you can. That's not why I'm offering." The woman popped the croissant into a second bag. "Consider it a welcome to Akaroa. I hope you enjoy your stay." She passed over the bag, and waved away Maddy's collection of coins. "So, have you traveled far?"

"From Amsterdam, via the US."

"That's about as far as you can get!" The woman tilted her head to one side. "So you're going to be sight-seeing for a few months?" She laughed. "I'm not sure we have that much to offer!"

Maddy was dying to take a bite out of the pie, but restrained herself. The woman was kind. She shrugged. "I thought I'd look around for a job. I have a temporary work visa," she added quickly, accustomed to people wary of illegal employment.

"What is it you do?"

She swallowed hard, trying to stop her mouth from watering. "Anything. I can wait at tables, answer phones. I know a few languages, and I've done barista work. I can turn my hand to anything." One more inhalation of the pie and she couldn't wait any longer. She took a bite and closed her eyes as the flavors of the meat pie filled her mouth.

The woman cocked her head to one side. "Really? I'd have put you down for something brainy like, I don't know, something hard and sciency."

Maddy nearly choked at the woman's accurate observation. She swallowed, and then coughed.

The woman grinned. "I'm right, aren't I? I'm always right about people. My sisters reckon I have a sixth sense." She stuck out a hand. "I'm Amber."

Maddy gripped the hand. "Madeleine MacGillivray, but everyone calls me Maddy. It's lovely to meet you, Amber."

Amber moved around the counter and hesitated. Maddy braced herself for more questions. Amber didn't strike her as the kind of woman who worried too much about privacy. The inquisition was about to begin. She mentally rehearsed her answers to how she knew about Akaroa and what had drawn her here for more than just a brief visit. Instead Amber gestured to the coffee machine. "Would you like a coffee to go with that pie?"

Maddy let a long breath escape. "That would be great. It's been a long time since the plane."

"So... you've just arrived in today."

"Yeah. I'm pretty tired. They were longer flights than I imagined."

"It's the price you have to pay for living in paradise." Amber smiled again and poured two coffees. "Mind if I join you for five minutes?"

"Sure," said Maddy surprised, as she followed Amber to a nearby table.

"So tell me, what kind of job are you looking for?"

"Anything really. Recently I've worked in hotels—cleaning, admin, reception, whatever is required." It was on the tip of her tongue to tell Amber what her real profession was. But that was too much, too soon. "So..." Maddy looked around the café, desperate for a change in subject. "Is this your café ?"

"No. I just work here. It gives me enough money to allow me to follow my passion."

"Which is?"

"Art. I love creating things. Installations, paintings, sculpture, glasswork. You name it, I'll have a go at creating it."

"That's amazing. I'm always in awe of artists. I can't imagine how they can come up with things. The few times I've tried, it looks like a child has created it. Actually, I'm doing children a disservice. But it looks nothing like I imagine."

"I guess there's a place for all of us, isn't there?" Amber grinned. "I don't know of any waitressing jobs going. Is there anything else you could turn your hand to? I know someone who needs help with office work."

"Accounts, that sort of thing? Sure. I know spreadsheets inside out."

Amber slammed her hand on the table, making Maddy jump. "I have just the job for you! This person needs help; he's hopelessly disorganized, paperwork everywhere. I reckon probably everyone in the town owes him money." She jumped up. "Stay there. I have a phone call to make."

Maddy didn't need further persuading and began to make serious in-roads into the pie. The food and coffee soon improved her spirits and, when Amber slid into the seat opposite again, unable to suppress a grin, Maddy felt cautiously optimistic.

"I've got you a job!"

"You've got me a what?"

"A job! Or an interview for one. I have to warn you that he doesn't think he needs help, but at least he's agreed to see you." She giggled. "I put a sign on his door last night. I try it from time to time. I wonder if it's still there. It usually doesn't last long." She sat back with a self-satisfied smile. "And somehow, I reckon he'll take one look at you and be more than happy to employ you. And not just because it'll take the pressure off him from the family."

Maddy couldn't quite bring herself to match the brightness of the smile. Amber's implication that this man would employ her based on her looks alone made her feel uncomfortable. "What can I say? Thank you so much."

"No problem. Now, do you have anywhere to stay?"

Maddy shook her head and waited. Somehow she thought Amber might have a solution to this problem too. She didn't have to wait long. Amber scribbled something on the back of the café's business card and pushed it across the table with a triumphant look. "There's a small backpackers' hostel down the road. It's run by Floriana—although only call her that if you want a black look—and if you care to help out there I'm sure she'll give you a good deal." She plucked one of the postcards that sat on the table and scribbled a note. "Take this to Flo."

Maddy took the note from her, noting the beautifully formed words. "Not many people write notes, now."

"I don't use cell phones. They destroy the atmosphere."

Maddy grinned. "You mean the radio waves?"

Amber shrugged. "No, just the atmosphere. It feels better without them. The vibe is different."

Maddy looked around the small café and had to agree. The vibe of the café was peaceful. And Amber was most definitely unusual. "I think I'm going to like it here."

"Good. Akaroa could always do with more permanent residents."

Maddy suddenly felt alarmed. "Oh, I'll be gone by winter." She bit her lip to stop herself from saying anything further.

Amber tilted her head to one side. "Like a migrating bird."

The doorbell jangled, and she finished her coffee. "Enjoy your breakfast, I'd best get on."

Amber bounced across the café to serve another customer, her red ponytail swinging down the back of her black t-shirt. Maddy took another bite of her pie and looked out the window across the harbor, calm and unruffled under the morning sun, toward the far hills. And she suddenly realized that, for the first time since he'd died, she felt soothed. Whether it was the town itself, cradled in the hills next to such a beautiful harbor, or Amber's warmth and generosity, or the fact that it was his hometown, she couldn't have said. The pie was also a contender, she thought, as she took another bite. She hadn't realized how hungry she was. She finished the pie and decided to save the croissant until later. She didn't know when she'd be eating again. She drank the last of her coffee and returned the mug to Amber.

"Thanks so much for everything. You've been very kind."

"I hope you enjoy your stay, Maddy, however long you decide to make it. It's peaceful here and, if you don't mind me saying, you look as if you could do with a little peace."

Maddy raised her eyebrows in surprise. She wasn't in the habit of communicating with strangers, and she'd said more to Amber than usual. There was something about the petite redhead that seemed to make small talk pointless.

"All the best with the job, and Flo."

"Thanks." She pulled the rucksack onto her shoulder. "So, when is my interview for the job?"

"He usually comes here for lunch. He's a creature of habit. Be here at one, and you'll see him. And after six, he'll probably be eating his usual chips or whatever in the local pub, or at his house. You'll be able to catch him there later if it's easier." She scribbled down the address.

Maddy didn't look at the card, just slipped it into the back of her rucksack. "Thanks so much for everything. I didn't expect to have found food, a job and a place to stay within the first hour of my arrival!"

Amber laughed and, disconcertingly, stepped forward and gave Maddy a hug. It was just a brief one, but it shocked her. She did her best not to get close to people. Looking like she did, most people felt she was aloof, standoffish, and she didn't do anything to contradict that impression. But for some reason, Amber wasn't to be put off.

Maddy stepped back. She could see in Amber's eyes that she had registered Maddy's shock, and Amber smiled reassuringly. "I'll see you at lunchtime then."

"Sure," said Maddy, fiddling with the straps on her bag. "Sure," she repeated, standing up straight and forcing a smile on her face. She hated being touched. It made her feel vulnerable.

Amber's grin widened. "Give me one more 'sure,' and I'll begin to doubt you."

Maddy's forced smile turned into a natural one. It seemed Amber wasn't to be put off by anything. She was a force of nature. "I'll see you later." She hitched her rucksack onto her back

"Maddy!" Amber called. Maddy turned around. Amber had followed her and was leaning against the counter, her arms crossed, watching her.

"Yes?" She wondered for a terrible moment if she'd misunderstood and owed some money after all.

"Why are you here? Sorry, I'm curious."

Maddy kept herself to herself, and always had done, until she'd met him on a rainy afternoon in Amsterdam and he'd teased her out of her shell. But she was firmly back in it again now. However, she owed this woman the truth, or at least a part of it. "I'm keeping a promise to someone."

Amber frowned. "Sounds intriguing."

Maddy shrugged. "Not really. It's just a promise." Maddy hoped that Amber would leave it at that.

"Promises are important. Anyhow, have a great day and say 'hi' to Gabe for me."

Gabe? Amber hadn't mentioned the person's name before and, as Maddy walked out the door, the name stuck in her head. She felt for the card, but it was zipped up tight and out of reach. She must have put it in the back pocket of her rucksack. She'd check later. Gabe? She repeated it to herself. It wasn't an unusual name, she supposed. Gabriel, Gabe. But still.

Maddy closed the door quietly, trying to minimize the brassy jangle of the bell which cut through the quiet of the early morning. She walked down the steps of the café and across the road so she could enjoy the beauty of the harbor on her walk to the backpackers' which was situated at the farther end of a curve of the bay. A light mist lay on the water which was a soft grayish green, reflecting the color of the hills on the far side of the harbor and the diffused light in the sky above. There was not a breath of wind: it was as if the morning was holding its breath, waiting to see what would come of Maddy MacGillivray's visit to the other side of the world. She was beginning to feel curious, too, now that she'd eaten and regained some courage. Which was just as well, she reflected, because she sure needed courage now.

She looked around for a bench or table, hidden from sight of the café. She needed to be somewhere private before checking. She found a lone bench under the shade of a pohutukawa tree. She swung her heavy rucksack onto the wooden seat, sat down beside it, and pulled out the card. She looked across the sweep of the bay toward the opposite side of the harbor. It had a pale, early morning gleam which reflected the light too brightly, making it hard to see beyond the surface. The colors of the hills, the pier jutting out into the water and the line of colonial houses behind her which edged the beach road, were affected by the bright gleam, taking the edge off the color, bleaching it with its brilliance. It felt strangely unreal, tapping the card in her hand as her mind returned to Amsterdam and her last moments with the man who'd cast a spell on her. He was gone now, but the spell remained.

He'd told her to come. He'd told her she had to stay for six months; he'd told her to seek out Gabe. Was this the same man? How could it be? What sort of world was it that everything lined up neatly for her? Not the sort she was used to, for sure. But ever since she'd landed in New Zealand things seemed to have fallen into place. She'd been met with nothing but friendliness and kindness—particularly in Akaroa, particularly with Amber.

So. She tapped the card, drew a deep breath and turned it over in her hand. "Gabe Connelly" it read.

She sucked in a jerky breath. Dr. Gabe Connelly. She bit her lip as she slid the card back in her pocket. She'd thought she'd come here, stick around for the six months she'd promised, and make a desultory attempt to make contact with Gabe Connelly, just as she'd promised to do. But not do anything more than that. Looked like fate had other ideas.

2

Dr. Gabriel Connelly finished his phone call after listening to yet another lecture from his little sister, Amber.

Gabe had always found that it didn't pay to argue with Amber because (a) she never let logic stand in the way of her opinions, and (b) she was usually right. It *was* time he employed someone to do his accounts for him. Although how Amber deduced this was beyond him. He knew for a fact that Lizzi took care of all of Amber's finances after discovering that if Amber had managed her money better—particularly if she hadn't given half of it away to anyone with a sob story—she'd have been able to put down a deposit on an apartment. No, it wasn't only Amber; it was another Connelly Sister Conspiracy. He really should call it the CSC for short—it happened often enough.

His sisters—Lizzi, Rachel, and Amber—had an uncanny instinct when it came to knowing what their brothers needed. Gabe imagined them texting and phoning each other daily to check out whether any of their brothers—or Dad, he wasn't exempt from their meddling—needed advice, guidance, help or downright interference in their lives. Since Max was married he was out of the picture—he didn't think Laura would take kindly to sisterly intrusion—and his other two brothers, Rob and Cameron, were overseas, so the CSC had upped the ante on Gabe. Gabe just hoped it wouldn't take something drastic like marriage to make his sisters believe that he was okay.

He tossed his phone onto the couch and looked out onto the main street of Akaroa. He loved this place, despite, or (he had to admit) because of his family. Every time he returned from an overseas stint for *Médecins Sans Frontières* his appreciation of his home went up a notch.

Amber teased him that one of these days he'd return to Akaroa and never leave. But she was wrong. Yes, it was his home, where he and his family lived, but that wasn't enough for him. It was all too easy; *he* was easygoing, and there was nothing he could do about that. The quiet town had few dramas, and well, not to put too fine a point on it, he wanted something more to exercise his restless mind. He'd had a few relationships before becoming engaged to a woman some years before. He'd called it off when he realized that he didn't feel as strongly for her as she did for him. Even now the word "love" didn't enter his head when he remembered his ex-fiancée. She'd been lovely, comfortable, an easy companion, but there had been something missing. And he had no idea what. But it had warned him off women for some time. He didn't want to hurt anyone and until he felt sure he wouldn't, and until he could understand them better, he reckoned he needed to stay clear.

He was about to turn away from the window to check his diary when a flash of white caught his eye. A young woman—tall, scruffily dressed and wearing a heavy-looking rucksack—looked first one way and then the other and walked quickly across the road to avoid a car. He caught a glimpse of wide blue eyes, high cheekbones and a spare bone-structure revealed by the blonde ponytail which swung down her back as she twisted to check the traffic. She was stunning, and there was something about her manner which looked as if she either didn't have the first idea how gorgeous she was, or, if she did, she couldn't have cared less.

He let out a slow whistle under his breath. He might not understand women, he might not be dating, but he could still appreciate a beautiful woman when he saw one. His eyes lingered on her as she hesitated on the corner of the street, and looked up at the hills that rose above Akaroa, bright in the early sunshine. He inhaled slowly, trying to quiet his quickened heartbeat, trying, in vain, to damp down his instant attraction to this stranger, because she wasn't only beautiful, she had a different quality about her, something he couldn't pin down, something out of place. There were plenty of beautiful people passing through Akaroa, from rich boaties popping in for coffee before taking off to their secluded holiday homes, to scruffy back-packers like this woman, but she looked different. And he couldn't put his finger on why. She was a stranger with a story. He felt it in his bones. He groaned. God save him from mysterious women with stories. But he knew, if God was on his side, he wouldn't save him from her, he'd help him get to know her.

His brief prayer to God was interrupted by the buzzer of his intercom, and his elderly receptionist's voice loudly announced his next patient as if she were presenting the news on the BBC World Service. He smiled to himself. After a year Brenda still couldn't get used to the intercom. He opened the door, grinned at Brenda who sat immaculate in pearls and suit, and ushered his next patient inside.

As he listened to his patient, all thoughts of the mystery blonde disappeared. He loved his patients and he loved helping them. They always received one hundred percent of his attention. For now, at least.

The Backpackers' Lodge was closer than Maddy had imagined. It seemed nowhere was far from anywhere else in Akaroa.

The two-story colonial weatherboard house took up half a block between the road and the beach. Public access was through a side door while the front door appeared to open onto a large private garden which ran up to the road. Maddy knocked on the side door but when there was no answer, she followed the sound of voices around the back where a large veranda opened directly onto the beach, complete with comfy old chairs and rickety table whose varnish was chipped with the salt air.

It wasn't peak holiday season yet, but even so, sandy jandals littered the porch, and towels hung limply over the railings. Early risers were already sitting out on the veranda, eating, drinking coffee and quietly talking. Maddy thought the crate of empty beer bottles at the bottom of the veranda steps probably accounted for the subdued manner.

"Hi!" said a woman, before taking a sip of coffee.

"Hi," said Maddy, with a brief smile which faded as the woman's companion eyed her up and down. Maddy was wearing her usual khaki shorts and faded checked shirt over a t-shirt. Feeling self-conscious, she eased her rucksack off her back. She nodded once more at the girl. "Is it okay to go on in? I'm looking for Floriana—I mean Flo."

The girl laughed. "Floriana? Is that her name? No wonder she refused to tell us!"

Maddy groaned. She'd probably alienated Flo already.

"She'll be in or around the office at this time of day."

"Thanks," said Maddy. She walked through the open

French doors into a communal sitting room and went through to a wide hallway to find people everywhere with a woman in their midst who emanated calm and control. She was of medium height, of more than medium build but with an air of authority which everyone surrendered to. And, when she looked up, Maddy noted that she also had the most beautiful green eyes she'd ever seen. One by one people followed the woman's lead, stopped talking and stared openly at Maddy. She tried to look shorter, more insignificant, to hide in her travel-worn clothes, but it made no difference. She addressed the woman at the center of the group, who she assumed to be Flo. "Hi, I'm Maddy. Are you Flo?"

"Yes, I am. Hi Maddy. Are you looking for a place to stay?"

"Yes, I met Amber at the café. She said you might have a bed free and that I might be able to help out."

Flo didn't look convinced. "And what kind of help can you give us?" Doubt was evident in every deliberate syllable.

Maddy was also used to that. "Anything you want. I can cook, make beds, keep house, do the accounts."

"Accounts?" Flo's look of skepticism turned to admiration. "You know about spreadsheets?"

Maddy's mouth twitched. "Sure do. Love 'em. They're my favorite software."

Flo's wary expression disappeared under a broad grin. "I've never heard anyone say that before. I'm afraid I can't pay you. Is a free room okay instead? It'd only be a few hours a day, maybe more to begin with to get to grips with it all."

Maddy was both relieved that she had somewhere to stay and amused that everyone she'd met in Akaroa so far had an aversion to spreadsheets. "That would be great. Amber's arranged an interview for me with the doctor, to help him out. I'm hoping he'll pay rather than give me free medical advice."

Flo grinned. "He'll probably give you both. Come on, I'll show you your room. It's a single, so you won't have to put up with partying teenagers. Better give me a few phone numbers for references, to make sure you won't run away with our paltry earnings."

"Sure."

"And maybe you could help me out around the hostel as well? My cleaner has gone AWOL. If you can lend me a hand this morning, I'll show you the accounts tomorrow? How does that sound?"

Madeline grinned and shook her head in disbelief that everything was falling into place so smoothly. "Perfect!"

It was Flo's turn to laugh. "See if you still think it's perfect after a morning changing sheets and cleaning rooms!"

AFTER A MORNING'S HOUSEWORK, Madeline did still feel the same. Working in the homely hostel was nowhere near as bad as working in hotels, as she'd been doing the past year. With everything in order, Maddy slipped outside into the garden and found Flo tending some herbs. The large, well-designed garden was full of color and was evidently something of an obsession with Flo. Flo looked up and thrust a bundle of tender leaves under Maddy's nose.

"Don't these smell amazing?"

The distinctive scent of coriander filled Maddy's senses. "Wonderful!"

"I've been trying to grow it from seed for a while. This is the first season it's taken off."

"You're a keen gardener, then?"

"I'm a keen gardener, cook, and decorator of houses—given the money, that is." She indicated the house. "I guess you could call me a homemaker."

Maddy was impressed. She couldn't imagine being so

happy in a home. She'd spent most of her life avoiding being tied down to one. "That's cool."

To her surprise, Flo grinned. "I doubt you believe that. Look at you. You look like you've just stepped out the pages of Vogue—albeit in a feature on how to dress to *not* stand out among the locals—and your resumé lists academic jobs, the titles of which I don't even understand. I seriously doubt that you think homemaking is cool."

"No!" Maddy was horrified that Flo would think she looked down on her. "No, really, I think being a homemaker is wonderful, and I envy you. And to know what makes you happy, well it doesn't get any cooler than that."

Flo put down her trowel and stood up, brushing the soil from her shorts. "Trouble with being a homemaker is that it doesn't pay, so I turned the home into a business." She glanced at Maddy. "And not a very profitable one at that, as I'm sure you've guessed from the state of the house. I only get the students because I keep the tariff so low. Too low." She shook her head and looked around the garden. "I love this place and yet I don't know how I can continue staying here. I haven't the heart to sub-divide the section."

Maddy followed Flo's gaze around the parterre garden, which was sheltered by towering linden trees, their fresh green leaves flashing in the sea breeze. Low buxus hedges and gravel paths divided the different sections of the parterre which contained a profusion of flowers—white daisies, tall foxgloves, delicate wildflowers and robust annuals—and a weeping pear tree grew at its center. There was a formal herb and vegetable garden closer to the house, and white wrought-iron chairs and a table were grouped under the shade of a cherry tree.

Flo sighed as her gaze rested on the house itself, through whose open windows you could see, and hear, the sea.

"It's too ramshackle for people wanting a weekend

getaway, and too far from the action for the cheap and cheerful crowd," she continued.

"There must be some in-between market which will pay to come here. I know I would."

Flo looked at her thoughtfully. "And what kind of crowd are you a part of?"

Maddy shrugged. "The kind which isn't impressed by luxury, but which values beauty and nature."

"So, are there more of you out there?" Flo grinned.

"There's got to be," laughed Maddy. "I can't be the only one!"

Flo rose and tapped her finger against her lips. "Then all we have to do is find them." The sound of the side-door bell ringing made Flo push herself off the wall and peel off her gardening gloves. "That'll be a few more waifs and strays looking for accommodation. The main backpackers must be full already."

Maddy followed Flo into the house and looked around with an assessing eye. It wasn't so much that it was falling down. The structure appeared pretty solid, but it needed paint and maybe wallpaper and some less shabby furniture to make the most of the house. It must have been grand once. There was a library at the rear, which opened into the garden. It was here that Flo lived and slept if the place got full. It was a beautifully proportioned room and still had the built-in bookshelves complete with columns whose plaster-work was coming away. Maddy shook her head. There was nothing that an investment of money wouldn't solve. If only she could help, but how? Maddy hadn't worked in her profession for years and had no family and few friends to call on after having cut ties with them two years earlier. As Maddy finished off her morning's work by putting the laundry on the washing line, she felt frustrated that she couldn't do something. But that wasn't why she was here, was it?

By mid-day, Flo was back out in the garden again, and Maddy was ready to meet Dr. Gabriel Connelly.

"I'll see you later, Flo!"

Flo looked up from trimming the lavender bushes. "So, you're off to meet Gabe?"

"Yes. Amber said he goes to her café for lunch every day."

"Yeah. Our Dr. Gabe is a creature of habit, loves his community and loves his family."

Maddy tried not to show her surprise, but Flo's wry arched eyebrow made her suspect that she'd failed. "He's married then?"

"No. Not married, much to the frustration of half the population of the surrounding district. No, what I mean is that he loves his family. That's why he goes to the café every lunchtime."

Maddy frowned. "How is that connected?"

"Didn't you know? Amber is Gabe's sister."

Maddy's heart sank further. Fate wasn't just taking a hand, it was scooping her up and dumping her in the middle of a Connelly spider's web. She just hoped she'd be able to extricate herself after the six months was up.

DR. GABRIEL CONNELLY emerged from his house straight onto the pavement of the main road in Akaroa. As he passed the entrance to his surgery, which he'd had built as an extension to his house, he plucked the last piece of card that had remained stuck to the door. It must have been Amber who'd put it there, and there *would* be words. Again. He loved his sister dearly but sometimes he wished she'd stop interfering in his life. Still, if this backpacker could tell an invoice from a statement, he'd hire her. At least it would get Amber and Rachel off his back.

With the morning's surgery over he was free to enjoy fresh sea air—a definite improvement on the smell of disinfectant which lingered in his consulting rooms—and meet his sister, and whoever else of his family was around in the café where she worked. His family teased him about his routine. His big brother Max in particular. Max wasn't happy unless he was doing something death-defying with his adventurous wife, Laura. The idea of leading a 'small life' as Max described it brought Max out in a sweat. But Gabe never rose to the bait. Max's 'big' life didn't hold any interest for him.

No, Gabe was more aware than most of the problems in the world, making him appreciate the quality of life he had in Akaroa. It was comfortable, it was easy, and it was useful—more than the majority of the world's population could say.

But, on that sunny summer morning, Gabe stopped dead in the street as an apparition walked along the end of the road, looking out to sea. Correction, the apparition glided by. It was the young woman he'd seen earlier. She must have been all of six foot, as slender as a willow, and as blonde as something very blonde. Cars slowed as they passed by, a couple of road workers whistled, but she didn't look around, didn't seem to notice. But everyone else did. The apparition disappeared as she continued along the beach front. Gabe picked up his pace. Following beautiful women wasn't something he'd ever done before but in this case it appeared that they were headed in the same direction, so he reckoned it was okay.

He frowned as the apparition stopped at Amber's café and went inside where Amber greeted her warmly. She couldn't be! Fate didn't work out like this for him. He followed her into the café and watched as she went where Amber indicated, back outside through another door to a table on the pavement. It was his favorite table, the one Amber always kept free for him.

He raised an eyebrow in query at Amber, and she grinned and nodded. He followed the apparition—who now had a name—to the table and stopped in front of her.

"Hi!" he said. "You must be Madeleine." He stuck out his hand.

She rose awkwardly, and the chair nearly fell back, but she caught it just in time. "Maddy, please. And you must be Dr. Connelly." She took his hand in greeting and blushed. He liked that.

"Yes, I am. Amber said you were interested in a job, and that you have years of experience working as an accounts clerk." Even as he said it, he wondered whether Amber was spinning him another line. Truth and Amber didn't necessarily always go together. Sometimes a story, or an intention, won out over reality. She said in her defense that it made life just a bit nicer. Again, hard to argue with.

Maddy grimaced and shrugged apologetically. "That's a little on the, well..."

It looked like this woman was a bit better acquainted with truth than Amber. "Untrue side?" he prompted.

"Yeah. But I *do* know spreadsheets."

"*I* know spreadsheets. They're those computer programs with lots of squares."

"Yes, but I *really* know them, and *really* like them. I can do things with spreadsheets that you wouldn't believe."

"I bet you're right." She had his imagination in overdrive, and he wanted to see this in action.

"I am. So if you'll give me a chance, say a few days, I'll look at your accounts, and if you're not happy with my work, I'll leave."

"Sounds fair enough. I guess you have some references?"

"Yes, of course." Again that doubtful look.

"But not from accountants."

She pulled an apologetic face. "No, more from universities."

"Universities? Did you work in admin?"

Maddy shook her head. "Archaeology."

His eyebrows shot up in surprise. "Archaeology? Amber didn't say anything about that."

She shrugged. "I don't think I mentioned it." She looked distinctly uncomfortable. It was obvious she didn't want to talk about her work. "I've managed quite large grants, so I'm sure you'll find I'm trustworthy."

"I don't doubt it. If Amber trusts you, then who am I not to?" He grinned.

"So, Dr. Connelly—"

"No! Not Dr. Connelly. Gabe. Please call me Gabe. And not Dr. Gabe. *Especially* not Dr. Gabe. It makes me feel like someone off a reality TV show." His brows lowered in mock seriousness. "Dr. Gabe... family doctor, but can you trust him?" he said in a voice that the best voiceover actors would have envied.

Her lips tweaked into the beginnings of a smile. "I reckon I can trust you. Pleased to meet you, Gabe."

He'd never heard his name sound so sexy on a woman's lips. "And very pleased to meet you. I'm in need of someone organized and efficient." He frowned. Could this wondrous beauty know her way around spreadsheets? "That *is* what you are, isn't it?"

She appeared to shake herself mentally and did something next for which he was unprepared. She smiled, and the sun came out. Literally and figuratively. It was like a curtain had been swept away from a window, revealing a glorious day. He tried to rein in an answering smile but failed.

"That *is* what I am," she agreed. "My mind seems to work differently to just about anyone else."

"If it works differently to mine, then that's a good thing." Again that grin, and his heart melted. He hadn't had such an instantaneous reaction to a woman in a long time. "You're hired."

Her soft sable brows shot up. "Hired? But you know nothing about me."

"Your name is Maddy, your mind works differently to mine, and Amber trusts you. What else do I need to know?"

She shrugged. "Maybe you should check out my references to make sure I'm not some maniac?"

"Sure. You can do that for me."

"You want me to check out my own references?"

"Yeah. If you get time after you've tried to sort out my paperwork."

She laughed.

"But before that, we need to eat. You'll need all your energy to sort out my invoicing system."

"So you *do* have a system, then?"

He grimaced. "If you can call handwritten notes on a spike a system, then yes, I have a system."

She laughed and shook her head. "Is everyone too busy, or too artistic to concern themselves with order and efficiency here?"

He nodded. "That's the inhabitants of Akaroa in a nutshell. Just as well you're here. You should stay. We need you."

The smile disappeared. He'd said something wrong, but he had no idea what. She turned away, and her curtain of hair swung with her, hiding her expression.

"Anyway," he continued, looking over at Amber. "Let's eat, and we can get to know each other before I open the doors and reveal my messy life."

He continued talking as they waited for Amber, disappointed that the brief bright ease had gone, robbed by something he'd said, and determined to make it reveal itself again.

They sat at his usual table outside on the street. He liked to sit out on the sidewalk where people could see him, and ask him about their ailments if they couldn't pay. Not that he'd have made them. The invoices for those who'd have struggled to pay would never have made it to the spike. But this lunchtime, he hoped that no one would stop and take his attention from the beautiful woman who sat opposite, looking a little uncomfortable and nervous. Not surprising considering most of the cafe was watching her. But she didn't meet anyone's eyes. No doubt some self-preservation instinct because she evidently didn't like the attention. Beautiful and unaware, he liked that. Then she turned to look out at the bay, and he could admire her face with its high cheekbones, and well-defined jawline and nose. It was a strong face, a spare face, no surplus flesh to mar or soften its edges, but it was also a sad face. This woman had suffered. For all the beauty of her sunshine smile, she wasn't happy. Damn. If there was anything more attractive to him than a beautiful woman, it was a sad and mysterious one.

"What will you have?" Amber asked, looking very pleased with herself.

"The usual, please." His sister had every right to look pleased; she'd introduced him to the kind of woman he adored, and she knew it. But it was pretty galling to have your love life arranged for you by your kid sister.

Maddy was scanning the menu. "The house salad, please."

"Is that all?" he asked. "That's not enough to keep body and soul together. And I was hoping you'd be working hard for me this afternoon."

"You're thinking about yourself, as usual," said Amber, with a smile.

"You know me."

"I do." They exchanged glances which said more than words.

"Gabe's right. Have something more than that." Amber looked around and bowed her head to Maddy's. "It has to be said our salads are pretty measly. I'd go for the veggie burger and chips if I were you. It's all home-made, no additives—I make sure of that."

"No, really, a salad's fine."

Gabe suddenly realized why Maddy had been so intently studying the menu. "I'm afraid I'm going to have to insist on paying. After all, this is a business lunch."

"But—"

He waved his hand. "No, I've got this. So please, how about making it something substantial like a burger and chips to make sure you have enough energy for the afternoon ahead?"

She shrugged, but smiled acceptance at Amber.

"Cool," said Amber, shooting an approving glance at Gabe.

Maddy watched her walk away before turning her blue-eyed gaze upon Gabe. "I've never met anyone like your sister before."

"Nor me. She's one of a kind."

She glanced at her with a look almost of longing. "I've always dreamed of having a sister like Amber."

It wasn't the first time that a woman he'd dated had said something similar, not only because they liked Amber, but because they were hinting at a future, the first sight of which made Gabe want to run.

But, with Maddy, there was no double meaning and no sense of flirtation. He was used to women who flirted without meaning what they said. And he was most definitely used to flirting back. But now it seemed this Goddess, who was made for flirting, had no interest in talking about anything superficial. He could do that. Possibly.

"Are you an only child, or do you have annoying brothers like Amber has?"

A dip in that lovely forehead and a downward glance was her first reaction. It was brief, but long enough for him to recognize the pain that lurked behind that immaculate façade. But it was gone when she looked up again. She knew how to hide her feelings.

"Only child," she said in that low, sexily accented voice of hers.

He grunted his thanks to Amber for the coffee she slid across the table and took a sip as he waited for Maddy to continue. "No doubt spoiled by your parents," he prompted. But even as he said the words, he somehow doubted it.

She gave a slight smile, but this time didn't take her eyes from his. "No. They died in a train accident in Europe; my uncle raised me."

"Spoiled by your uncle, then, I hope."

"Totally." She grinned, and he relaxed with relief. He couldn't bear the thought that someone hadn't spoiled this woman. If she'd answered in the negative he might have had to take on the task himself.

"Excellent. Everyone should have someone in their life who spoils them."

"He's not in my life anymore."

Gabe's heart sank. He added a spoonful of sugar to his coffee. He knew he shouldn't, but he needed it now, as he felt that old familiar feeling of needing to care for someone wash over him. "I'm sorry."

But to his surprise, Maddy smiled. "It's okay. We had a brilliant life together. He was an archaeologist and took me around the world to different archaeological digs. It was how I got into GIS."

"GIS?"

Her smile widened. "Geographic information systems. You've probably heard of it."

Gabe grinned. "Heard of it, yes; understand it?" He shook his head. "No."

"It's about the processing of geographic data which results from archaeology. We collect the data, store it, and retrieve it to create new information. That's the wiki version anyway."

"Well, thank you for giving me the wiki version. My scientific knowledge is confined to the human body; mathematics and statistics aren't my thing."

"I reckon it's the most important part of archaeology," she said with a disarming shrug of the shoulders. Talking about her work seemed to relax her.

"Of course. I don't doubt it. Although I'm sure the digging kind of archaeologists would dispute it."

"Oh, they do. But they don't win. You see, I have the facts and figures, and you can't argue with them."

"I have to side with the digging archaeologists there. I reckon there's more to an argument than 1s and 0s, bit and bytes, positive, negative."

"Ah, now, I don't want to argue with someone who's just bought me lunch."

"Good plan. I might refuse to pay."

"In which case I'd have to run away, again."

It was his turn to frown. He pushed the food around on his plate for a moment, and when he looked up, her expression had changed. She looked nervous again as if she'd said too much. He set down his knife and fork and folded his arms on the table, his eyes level with hers, challenging her to be open. Instead, she took a bite of her burger. He let the silence continue until she'd swallowed, but she still didn't elaborate. It was up to him to find out.

"Why are you here?"

She shrugged. "It's a beautiful place. Why not?"

"Because something tells me you seldom do things on a whim."

"Do you know people so well, after such a short time?"

"I have good instincts. They tell me the basics."

She hesitated as if fighting with herself and then sighed. "And what are your instincts telling you?"

"I don't need instincts to tell me that you have a reason to be here. You're right. Akaroa is a beautiful place, but people don't come here straight here off the plane. They stay in the cities, check out the main attractions, a few boiling mud pools in the North Island, some glaciers in the South Island. But you? You came straight to Akaroa, and intend to stay for a few months. And I'm wondering who told you about it."

She bit her lip and glanced away, as if in confusion. She took a deep breath and met his gaze once more with a lifted chin and courage she'd summoned up from somewhere deep. The thought that his presence unnerved her was a strange one. But now her face was blank and guarded. He wondered what he'd have to do to make her drop her guard. He wouldn't usually have pressed her for information, but he couldn't help himself; he wanted to know.

"Sorry, I don't mean to pry, but I'm curious about what it is you're looking for," he continued. "Something, or maybe someone?" he added as an afterthought. He wondered which would win out: the courage or the confusion.

Her gaze shifted, and she licked her lips. "You underestimate the charms of this place. I heard about it overseas and decided I had to come here and see for myself."

The courage had won. "I don't underestimate anything, Miss Madeleine MacGillivray. In fact, I'm known for it." His tone was purposely light, regaining the flirtation of their previous conversation. There was no sense pushing her into an uncomfortable place. That was a sure-fire way to turn her away from him. And, if there was one thing which he knew from their brief time together, it was that he didn't want her to turn from him.

She picked up his change in direction and went with it. "Is that right?"

"Yes, it is," he said. "Now, I think we've had enough of talking about you. You eat, and I'll talk, and I can tell you all about myself. Of course, you can tell me something about yourself if you have to."

She laughed, and the whole of the café turned to look for its source. Double damn. The sound was like a golden thread that tightened around his heart, making him gasp a little.

"No, you're fine," she said. "I'd prefer to talk about you."

"Excellent. Because, as it so happens, it's my favorite subject." He lied. But sometimes it was necessary.

MADDY ENDED up eating not only a veggie burger and chips in addition to the salad she'd ordered, but also a bowl of fruit salad and ice-cream. And Gabe's rationale for the big lunch had been scrapped as the lunch turned from one hour into two. His accounts could wait another day.

Maddy couldn't remember the last time she'd eaten or talked so much. Because, despite his protestations, Gabe had talked very little about himself. Instead, after putting her at her ease, he'd turned the conversation around back to her. And she hadn't even noticed until now, until their long lunch was over and Amber had begun to make shooing noises to get them to leave the otherwise empty café. Because it wasn't until now that she looked into his eyes and knew that, despite all her best intentions, she'd revealed herself, and he'd liked what she'd revealed. She'd thought he was easy and straightforward. But, contrary to first impressions Dr. Gabriel Connelly was neither of those things.

She'd have to be careful if she was to keep on track. She was fulfilling a promise to someone, that was all. Fulfil the promise and then leave. That was how it had to be.

3

After an evening listening to overseas students talk, sing, and strum guitars on the veranda, Maddy's evening had ended abruptly as jet-lag had hit her. She'd fallen into a dreamless sleep from which she didn't awake until dawn. For a moment she'd wondered where she was, and she jerked her head toward the light which edged the ill-fitting curtains, instantly alert. Then she remembered and relaxed against the pillow once more. She was where she was meant to be. And she didn't know what was in store for her, but at least the guilt and stress over postponing her visit was no longer with her. For good or bad, she was here, and she had to get on with it. With her body clock insisting it was evening, she rose, dressed and tiptoed out the sleeping house and onto the empty beach.

As dawn broke over the harbor, Madeline sat on the damp sand and reflected on the past twenty-four hours. Apart from sleeping, it was the first time she'd been alone—something which she hadn't anticipated. She'd thought she'd arrive, do what she had to do, and leave again six months later, barely having caused a ripple in this small town. But she hadn't counted on people being so friendly and welcoming. It was as if they'd opened up their lives, shuffled along a bit to make room for her, and then closed the curtains again. After twenty-four hours she was part of their world whether she wanted to be or not. And she didn't know how she felt about it.

She turned her gaze to the distant promontory covered in trees, above which she could see the chimneys and roof of a large house. Belendroit. It was Gabe's and Amber's family home. The Connelly homestead. She'd heard so much about it that it had attained something of a mythical status in her mind. She would go, just as she'd promised, but not yet. Maybe toward the end of her six-month stay, but not before. It would be too hard.

As she heard the sounds of life beginning in the hostel behind her, she rose and looked around once more. A hazy mist lay over the harbor, the hills on the far side rising colorless and ethereal. It was soft and seductive, but she couldn't let it seduce her. She mustn't.

"Hey! Maddy!" She turned to see Flo holding up two cups of coffee.

She grinned and ran up the sand to Flo and took a cup. "Thanks, that's so kind of you."

"Not kind at all," said Flo, taking a sip and narrowing her eyes against the glare of the first rays of sunshine, bright through the mist. "It's a lure to get you working. Follow me." Maddy followed Flo into the house and stopped at a door set under the stairs. "This is the cubby hole I like to call my office."

Maddy was relieved to see it was bigger than she'd first imagined. A room which Harry Potter would have been quite jealous of in fact, with its small window to the rear which looked out onto the back garden.

Flo opened a filing cabinet and tapped the tops of the folders.

"Here are all the receipts for expenditure." She slammed closed the old metal cabinet which must have been at least fifty years old and opened the second drawer. "And here's the paper trail for the income."

Maddy sipped her coffee and looked over Flo's shoulder, noting the clearly-labeled tabs on each of the files. "Cool. Looks like you've everything under control." She looked around. "So where's the computer?"

"Ah," said Flo with a grimace. "Ah," she repeated and sucked her lips. "Now that's where my system stops."

"Don't tell me you don't have a computer?"

"Oh no, I won't tell you that, because it wouldn't be true." Flo opened another smaller cabinet and pulled out an ancient laptop which looked like it weighed a ton. "Here's my answer to the modern tech world. Ta-da!" She offered it like a buried treasure, which it was.

"Good heavens!" Maddy took the laptop and opened it up gingerly. "I haven't seen anything like this since, since... well, to be honest, I saw one in a 'history of computers' exhibition in Amsterdam recently."

"You go to exhibitions called 'history of computers?'" Flo appeared to be more surprised by Maddy attending the exhibition than by the fact her computer had featured in one.

"Yeah, I love history of any kind."

Flo shook her head but stopped short of accusing Maddy of being weird. Maddy wouldn't have minded. It wouldn't have been the first time.

Maddy opened the laptop, and while it was charging took another sip of her coffee. "You can leave me to it if you have other things you need to do. I'll be fine."

A relieved-looking Flo took her at her word and closed the door, eager to leave the sight of accounts behind her.

Maddy ran her fingers along the keyboard, enjoying the feel of the familiar after such a long time.

It wasn't long before she'd forgotten where she was, and why she was here, and was absorbed in numbers, entering the figures from the paper copies, and creating a set of accounts on the spreadsheet.

By the end of the morning, she'd created a profit and loss spreadsheet which showed precisely how well the hostel was doing since Flo had taken over, or how badly, Maddy reflected, her gaze lingering on the minus figure in red at the bottom of the spreadsheet.

"These are great!" said Flo, her smile faltering as she looked at the bottom line.

"There's more to come. That's just the beginning."

"My accountant's going to love these. There's nothing for him to do, so his fees will come down. Thanks so much."

"After a week or so, there won't be so much for me to do."

"But you will stay, won't you? If the paperwork doesn't take too much time, how do you feel about continuing to help me out with some of the housework? I'll pay you for it. It'll save me finding someone else. That will leave me to get on with the garden. You can have the room for as long as you like. Deal?"

"Deal!" They shook hands and celebrated their partnership by sharing a slab of chocolate with a cup of tea.

"So you're off to Gabe's this afternoon?"

"Yes, he's going to show me around his accounting system."

Flo laughed. "System? Did he call it a system? If you think mine was bad, you should see his."

"That's okay. It makes it more of a challenge."

Flo looked astutely at Maddy. "Somehow I reckon a challenge to you would be insurmountable to the rest of us."

Maddy frowned. She hated it when people recognized

how smart she was. It made her feel even more of a misfit than she usually did. "You'd be surprised. I sometimes think the things that other people take in their stride are daunting to me. And things I find easy, for some reason other people put up barriers against."

Flo turned her gaze across the harbor, dropping her sunglasses back onto her nose. "Those damned barriers."

Maddy glanced at Flo but couldn't tell what she was thinking, and Flo had gone quiet. It looked like even the practical Flo had her issues. But somehow Maddy didn't think Flo would be confiding in her anytime soon. Flo struck her as someone who kept things close to her chest. That made two of them.

Maddy drained her tea and picked up the mugs. "I'd best be off now. I don't want to be late for my new boss."

"So many bosses, so little time," sighed Flo, also standing. "Not that I have a boss. Just the bank manager. But we all have those."

"I don't," said Maddy without thinking. She regretted it the instant Flo turned around, an incredulous look on her face.

"How do you manage without a bank manager?"

"The internet. I haven't been into a bank in years."

Flo shrugged. "We're pretty old-fashioned here. A bank is a person to us; an overdue invoice is a person, and a statistic is a person."

Maddy grunted. "They're figures on a spreadsheet in my world." She'd never really thought about it before, but that's what the world about her had become. Statistics. Nothing more real than that because otherwise, she might feel something. Seems keeping her promise was putting herself into the firing line of feeling. And that wasn't something she liked at all.

"Just as well you've come to my world for a while then. Might make you look beyond the statistic."

Maddy snapped around to face Flo, but Flo was continuing to put away some papers as if she hadn't just dropped a bombshell on Maddy. Flo's words sounded cutting, hard even, but Maddy was beginning to understand Flo a little. Flo spoke her mind and people could take it or leave it, but there was nothing underhand or bitchy about her. Maddy could deal with that.

"But not too much," Flo added. "I kind of like what you're doing for us!" She gave a cheery wave, not realizing she'd just given Maddy an almighty wake-up call, and disappeared upstairs to check the rooms. Maddy wondered, not for the first time, if there had been some secret purpose to the request she'd promised to fulfil.

MADDY HAD LEFT it till the last minute before arriving at the doctor's surgery. She wanted it to be business only. No lunch, nothing that would be difficult to handle. But there was no answer, so she had no choice but to go next door to where he lived.

The last thing she expected when she knocked on his door, was for it to be answered by a half-dressed doctor, wearing only jeans and a hastily pulled-on shirt which was unbuttoned, and rubbing his hair with a towel. A trickle of water ran down his chest from his hair.

"Hey," he said as he stood back, to allow her to enter the narrow hallway. "Sorry, about my state of undress, but I thought you were coming earlier, and then I thought I must have got it wrong and you were coming tomorrow. So I went to the gym and just got back."

"It's okay. No need to apologize." Although there was, but not for the reasons he thought. His chest was definitely responsible for diverting her attention. Her gaze slipped lower. And his muscled stomach, with the smattering of hairs, was inviting a hand to press against it. Yes, he needed to apologize for that, because she most definitely didn't want to see, or think the things, it was making her feel.

"I think there is." He waved her through to his study. "It's not exactly a professional way to begin our... our..." But words escaped him, too. He shrugged off the incomplete sentence.

She blushed at the omission of the word relationship. The very fact he couldn't say the word indicated that, despite her best efforts, this was becoming more personal than she wanted it to be.

"So," he said, picking up a cardboard box from the bottom of a cupboard. "Here it all is. I do all the paperwork at home. Well, the small amount I do do, I do here, at home."

His winning smile, combined with the chaos he held in his hands, broke the sexual tension, and she burst out laughing. She took the box and placed it on the desk.

"It's all yours," he said. "Can I get you a drink or anything?"

"No. I'm fine, thanks. I'll get on with the job." She looked around and saw a modern computer. "Thank goodness for the laptop. I'll make a list of any queries and come and find you when I've finished."

"You're a miracle worker."

"I haven't done anything yet."

"But you will. I can see it in your eyes. And," he said, backing out the door, "you're the only person who's looked at that box and agreed to help."

He closed the door behind him, and she picked up a few illegible scrawled invoices and wondered what she'd let herself in for.

. . .

By five o'clock she knew. The state of his accounts was worse than Flo's—although the bottom line was far healthier. There were unpaid invoices, consultations not charged for, even invoices paid for in kind, with meals, beer, other things which Gabe had apparently agreed to instead of payment. He was either hopelessly ineffective, or hopelessly kind and caring. Maddy suspected the latter. The rest of his business on the laptop proved he was efficient where he needed to be.

She looked through the window and saw him outside, talking on the phone. She hesitated, watching him, waiting until he'd finished, not wanting to disturb his call. He paced the small stone-flagged courtyard on tanned bare feet; his jeans were worn where they stretched against his thighs and elsewhere. She tore her gaze upward. His shirt was still hastily buttoned and open at his neck. It was an old shirt, white, with some faded blue pattern on it. But it wasn't his clothes that drew the eye. It was him. He had an appealing ease to his movements, he gesticulated while he talked, and had an infectious laugh. She had to face the fact that he had charm—bucket loads of it. He turned suddenly and met her gaze. She froze, embarrassed to be caught out. But his eyes and smile were warm, and he beckoned her outside.

She lifted the latch on the French windows and stepped outside. It was hot, and the fragrance of jasmine hung over chairs whose decrepitude had been partially covered with vivid pink paint. The courtyard was walled in on all three sides by neighbors, and as well as being on the phone, Gabe was also carrying on a conversation with his next-door-neighbor. His call wasn't as confidential as she'd imagined.

"Maddy, come and meet Fred. He keeps an eye on me."

A man, who must have been over eighty, popped his head around a tree and stuck his hand through the tangle of jasmine to her. "Pleased to meet you!"

She reached out and shook his hand. "You, too." She looked, bemused, from Gabe to Fred.

"Gabe tells me you're here to sort out his accounts," Fred said, in a north of England accent.

"Yes. It shouldn't take too long."

Fred coughed out a hollow laugh. "Either you haven't seen the full extent of his mess of papers, or you're a miracle worker."

"She's a miracle worker," said Gabe, finishing his call. "A miracle worker who'd no doubt like some refreshment. See you later, Fred."

"Only if you're lucky," Fred muttered and shuffled away.

"Would you?" Gabe asked her. "Like something to drink, I mean?"

"Yes, please. That would be great."

They got as far as the steps on to the small deck when there was a voice from the other side of the brick wall. A mop of gray curly hair was all that could be seen.

"Mrs. King!" Gabe greeted the hair. "I haven't seen you for a few days. Is everything all right?"

What followed was a long reply about every part of the woman's body. All her aches and pains were described in excruciating detail and, much to Maddy's surprise, Gabe let her talk.

After a while, the woman quietened down, and Gabe passed her a white long-haired cat which Maddy had assumed was his. It seemed the cat spent most of the time in his garden, no doubt appreciating the peace in Gabe's garden compared to the neighbor's, she thought.

As they returned indoors, she waited for Gabe to pass comment on his neighbors. But all he did was ask her whether she preferred a tea, wine, or beer.

"A beer would be great, thanks." She sat in the small

seating area the other side of the kitchen bench. Still, she waited, but he passed no comment. "Your neighbors…"

"Yes?" He passed her a beer from the fridge.

"They're very… friendly."

"Yeah. They're like family. Fred's a case. He knows everything about my life before I do." Gabe swigged his beer and didn't seem the least perturbed by the fact.

"And you don't mind?"

"No," he said, looking genuinely puzzled. "Why should I?"

She shrugged as she tried to figure out why he should. "Because… most people want privacy."

"Not me. My life is an open book. Whether I'm here, or overseas working, I like to know the people around me."

"You work overseas?"

"Yes. With *Médecins Sans Frontières* I travel a couple of times a year, mainly to Papua New Guinea. It's become a home away from home for me."

"I suspect everywhere you go is your home."

He frowned as he considered the matter, before looking back at her with surprised and interested eyes. "You may be right."

Gabe was one contented man. She'd never met anyone like him. "I don't have a home," she said.

Gabe looked shocked. "You must have."

"No." She laughed at his expression. "But it's fine. I don't want one either."

"Then you're not happy."

"I—" She couldn't continue because she didn't know how to reply. She couldn't remember the last time she'd asked herself that question.

"Maybe you should stop doing accounts and do the work you were trained in—computers"—he waved a hand—"and archaeology."

"Oh, I haven't done any archaeology for a while."

"Really? Why's that?"

She licked her lips as she tried to think of a reason which would satisfy, but which wasn't the truth. She failed. "I stayed put for a while. In Amsterdam, with a friend, and then afterward"—she shrugged—"I traveled."

"How come you don't need the money? Independent means?"

"No. I mean I stand to inherit some money from my uncle at the end of the year, but it won't be much. He didn't live the high life."

"He probably saved it all to leave to you."

"I doubt that."

"How come you don't know for sure? Most people would be dying to find out how much they're going to inherit."

"Not me. I haven't been in touch with my solicitor for some time."

"Ah, traveling around."

She took a swig of her beer and nodded. "And using up my funds. I'd been..." She hesitated again. Talking to Gabe was turning out to be a minefield. She'd been about to say "putting off coming," but that would only lead to more questions. "This is my last trip for a while. One last trip and then back to work in Europe, or wherever I can get a job."

"You might get one here."

She was silent. She might, but how to tell him that that was the very last thing she wanted? She grunted noncommittally.

"I can't imagine what that's like," Gabe said.

"What what's like?"

"One place being equally attractive, or unattractive, as the other."

"They're not all equal. Some universities have better research facilities, more interesting projects than others."

Gabe's smile faded to a gentle quirk on his lips. "I didn't mean that."

"What did you mean?"

"I meant not having a place you call home." He paused, but she looked away. She couldn't give him an explanation. Not now. Possibly not ever. "Where were you born?"

"Copenhagen. My father was from Scotland, and my mother, Danish."

"And you have no family there?"

"None that I know of. Possibly distant family." She shrugged. "Too distant to count."

"No family is ever too distant to count."

"Family means a lot to you, doesn't it?"

"Yes." A shadow fell over his expression as if thoughts of family weren't all happy ones.

"Well, it doesn't to me."

"You know," said Gabe, thoughtfully. "You should come to Belendroit and meet my family."

Maddy gasped and tried to cover it up with a cough, as she looked down at her beer, scraping the edge of the damp label aside with her nail. Belendroit! She'd never imagined she'd receive an invitation to visit there. She'd thought she'd turn up and knock on the door at the end of the six months. But an invitation? She felt a surge of panic as an alternative, very different, version of the future suddenly appeared before her. She couldn't let this new vision become a reality. "Why? Because you feel sorry for me because I don't have a family?"

He took a sip of his beer, but his narrowed eyes watched her. He didn't rush to answer, as if he was trying to figure her out. "I guess, yes."

"I'm fine." She tried to assume a bright and breezy manner, but she suspected if the creasing around his eyes were anything to go by, that she hadn't succeeded in fooling him.

"I'm sure you're fine. But"—he sat forward on his seat, and Maddy was taken aback once more by the power of his presence—"you know, 'fine' is a pretty mild kind of thing to be. If you find 'fine' satisfactory, I think feeling 'great' would blow your mind."

Maddy couldn't help imagining how Gabe could elevate her mood to 'great' and, once there, her mind refused to behave. She swallowed, embarrassment at her flushed cheeks making them flush even more. "I… I…"

He grinned. "Sorry." He sat back, and it was as if he'd pulled away from a caress, although he hadn't touched her. She took another nervous gulp of beer. "It's the curse of being a doctor. You can't stop trying to figure people out, and helping them."

"I'm fine," she repeated, wincing at her use of the word, which had never occurred to her as inadequate before. "I'm really okay." Even worse, she thought. "I don't need help."

"Sure. But the invitation still stands. Why not come tonight? Not everyone's home, but Rachel and Zane will be around, and my Dad. And you've already met Amber, although she probably won't be there. Rachel's a wonderful cook," he added, as if that might tip the balance.

Belendroit. Maddy knew the word was French for a beautiful place and it had always had the ability to conjure up something magical, a place of dreams. It had been spoken of so many times before that it had become almost mythical. And when she'd agreed to keep a promise to return to Belendroit, and get to know Gabriel Connelly, it had remained mythical. But now she was here, and it was reality. And it felt too much, too soon.

"The only scary thing about Belendroit are the dogs," said

Gabe, "Stanley and Boo are two very silly cocker spaniels who will try to lick you to death."

Maddy laughed. "It's a kind invitation, but I'd feel uncomfortable going to someone's family home who I don't know well."

"Okay." He crossed his arms and sat back and frowned. "How well do you have to know me before you accept the invitation?"

She laughed, relieved that he'd accepted her explanation. "I don't know, but I'm pretty sure it needs to be longer than twenty-four hours."

"There you go, again, reducing reality down to numbers."

She shook her head. "It's a fact."

"And another fact is that I'm always bringing strangers home to meet the family. They're used to it. You're nothing special, you know," he teased with a grin.

"That's good to know." It *should* have been good to know, but Maddy felt a rush of disappointment and was angry with herself.

"I thought it might make you feel more comfortable. It's not a date, nothing to make you feel ill-at-ease, just dinner with a large, noisy dysfunctional family, who happen to try to be on their best behavior around strangers."

She smiled. "You're creating an interesting picture of your family for me."

"How about I pick you up around six? Dad insists we eat early, despite Rachel trying to push the time later."

Maddy suddenly had a vision of arriving at Belendroit in Gabe's car, as if they were a couple. It was wrong, totally wrong. "No, thanks. Look, I appreciate the invitation, but I'd prefer not to."

"You shouldn't be shy. My family doesn't bite. Normally."

"I *am* shy, whether people bite or not. And, I'm sorry, I'd feel uncomfortable. I mean I hardly know you, and your family might jump to conclusions."

"Like what?" He grinned.

She shrugged. "I don't know, that there might be something between us."

"There is something which brings us together." Her heart nearly stopped as he stepped closer to her and reached down. His hand brushed hers as he picked up a bundle of receipts. She drew in a sharp breath. "These. You're good with figures, and I'm not."

"You know I don't mean that."

"Then what do you mean?"

She'd fallen into a trap of her own devising. She licked her lips. "That we're in a relationship." He opened his mouth to speak, but she shook her head, willing him not to interrupt. "And I have no desire to be in a relationship. I'll be leaving here in six months, alone."

To give Gabe credit, he barely missed a beat before continuing. "Fair enough. Message received and understood. So now that's out in the open, why don't we have some good platonic fun, with or without other people? Do some sightseeing, hang out and have a few beers. Make your months here enjoyable—great, even. What do you say?"

She grinned. She could accept those terms. They fitted with the promise she'd made, and they fitted with what she could do emotionally. "That does sound great."

"Even on those terms I still can't lure you to Belendroit?"

She shook her head firmly. "No, I'm sorry. I hope you understand."

It was clear from Gabe's face that he didn't understand. A cloud had descended. But she couldn't enlighten him. She couldn't explain why it would feel all wrong to go to Belendroit escorted by Gabe.

"Right," she responded, too quickly, suddenly anxious to

avoid any pregnant pauses—silences filled with unasked questions, and unacknowledged attraction. "So, I'd best be off now."

"Sure." He gave a subdued smile as if he understood, and gestured toward the front door. "After you."

They walked along the corridor to the front door, but even as she left the house and stepped out into the evening sunshine, the shadow hadn't lifted from Gabe's face. And she didn't know how to make that happen without revealing everything, and it was too soon to do that.

She'd made a promise which she'd vowed to keep until the six months were up. And then? She couldn't even begin to imagine how she was going to tell Gabe that the reason she was here was she'd made a promise to a man—and not just any man—but Gabe's twin brother, Jonny.

4

The days fell into a routine of sorts which Maddy found herself enjoying, despite everything she'd anticipated. She'd never been an early riser, but the smell of bacon frying had the same effect on her as on every other resident of The Backpackers' Lodge—nobody wanted to miss out on one of Flo's breakfasts.

People from all over the world came and went, some for a few days, some for longer, drawn by the beauty of Banks Peninsula and Akaroa Harbor. And breakfast was usually spent in conversation with the others until it was time to help clean the rooms and do the paperwork.

Then the morning was hers until she was due at Gabe's house at one in the afternoon. She'd set the time. She knew he'd be busy and he was. Some days she didn't even see him. Gabe had stuck to her request that they be friends only and hadn't made any advances toward her, for which she was grateful.

Despite the open window the heat refused to shift in the small cubby-hole of an office. The weather had become hotter in the weeks since she'd first arrived, and the guests at the Backpackers more plentiful, but the bottom line was still far from healthy. And Maddy had had no repeat invitation from Gabe. She should be happy—it made life more straightforward, except it didn't. Maddy sighed and tried to focus once more on Flo's business.

She could usually focus on anything, whatever the conditions. She'd been used to it after all. Whether it be a dig in Africa with her uncle, or much later, surveying the snowy wastes of the Russian Steppes, she'd always found it easy to switch off her physical responses and become absorbed in the mental. But not now, for some reason.

Instead, she drew abstract shapes with her middle finger on the mouse trackpad on the laptop, watching the cursor move around the neat cells of the spreadsheet, with their figures impeccably formatted, and sighed once more.

If only life were as simple as slotting things into boxes and having them all add up at the bottom. She slid her finger down, revealing the total at the bottom. Idly, she entered a few commands and created a graph with the figures.

Flo looked over her shoulder and gave an even heavier sigh. "That"—she pointed at the figure which didn't even need a comma to separate out the hundreds—"is not good." Then she looked at the graph where the line of her expenditure was barely discernible from her income.

Maddy raised her eyebrows in agreement but kept quiet. Flo was right. Maddy had no idea how Flo kept body and soul together on such a small sum.

Flo walked away, and looked out to her cherished garden, as if for consolation. "What am I going to do?" she asked quietly.

Maddy licked her lips. She'd given it a lot of thought since she'd come here but hadn't liked to make any suggestions unless asked. "I think you're catering to the wrong market."

Flo turned around, with a frown. "And what kind of

market, other than kids, are going to want to stay here?" She indicated the places where she'd painted over wood which desperately needed replacing. "Not anyone with a choice, that's for sure."

Maddy followed Flo into the main sitting room, still with its original features and lofty proportions. "You're wrong. This is a wonderful place, full of character."

"Full of badly patched walls, and wood."

"But look beyond that, and you see exactly what people come to Akaroa for—history, charm and peace. And apart from any of that, your house is located on the beach, for heaven's sake. You don't get better than that."

Flo glowered. "I'm not taking investors on to turn this place into some yuppy boutique hotel. There will be *no* cocktails on my watch."

Maddy laughed. "It's not one thing or the other. There's a middle ground of people who appreciate the real Akaroa, and the comforts of home that you offer."

The glower faded. "What kind of people?"

"People like me. People who have traveled and appreciate something real and authentic, something comfortable and elegant, something that resonates with stories and character."

Flo grunted. "People like you don't come along every day, you know. And besides, even people like you will want a bath that doesn't sound like someone's dying when the water drains out."

Maddy grinned. "True. But if you have a plan, then you can attract money to put these things in order."

"Right." But Flo didn't sound convinced. "What you haven't taken into account, is that I'm not the business-planning type. I don't know why I ever thought I could use my grandparents' home like this. They didn't even live in it for the latter part of their life. They refused to."

"But they also refused to sell it. They knew it was valuable and they had faith that you'd be able to make a living from it, to make it your home, too." Maddy flipped open a website and turned the laptop around to show Flo. "This is the kind of business you could create here. I'll help you if you like."

"And then what? What's the point, Maddy? I'll simply end up with a brilliant plan, and nothing to take it forward."

"What you'll end up with is a plan to sell to the bank, or someone with money. You need money, Flo, to make this work for you. Face it, you need a loan or preferably a business partner."

"Even if I did want one—which I most definitely don't—why would anyone be interested?"

"Because it's a potential gold mine. Besides the setting, the house, the garden—there's you."

"Me," said Flo, disbelief plastered across her face. "You think *I'm* the drawcard?"

"Absolutely." Maddy indicated the well-used books in the bookcases, which flanked the grandly carved fireplace, and the second-hand tables on which retro lamps cast an inviting light in the evenings. "*Things,* you can re-create, but *people,* you can't. The backpackers love coming here because of you. You make sure they have the kind of food even their mothers probably aren't skilled enough to give them, and you make sure they're comfortable. You call the doctor if needed. You give them a respite from the rough world of backpacking."

"And they pay a pittance in return."

"Exactly. You can't go on like that. You need to nurture people who will pay you a fortune for your efforts." Maddy realized she was getting a little carried away, which wasn't like her. "Well, at least a reasonable going rate."

Flo grinned. "A reasonable going rate. I like the sound of that."

"It's Saturday. I haven't any work at Gabe's so why don't we start working on this business plan?"

"And then what?"

"We'll worry about that later."

IT WASN'T until late afternoon that Maddy had finished work on a basic business plan. Flo had long since left her to it to get on with her never-ending list of things to do.

It was a good plan, even if Maddy said so herself. It wouldn't attract the wrong kind of investor; it would attract someone who wanted to enhance the community in keeping with Flo's vision, while making some money at the same time. She looked around the place. The trouble was, it wouldn't be small change that was needed.

Maddy stood and stretched, and wandered through the house and onto a veranda which overlooked the beach. It was where all the residents hung out. There were a number there now, one strumming a guitar, another lazing in a hammock. An English couple played Monopoly from a box which had seen better days and another group played cards compiled from different decks.

She greeted people and sat on an inviting beanbag next to a pile of books. She quickly found one of interest and was soon absorbed in the history of Akaroa. After reading several chapters she looked around with fresh eyes, interpreting the landscape with her new knowledge. There were round indentations the size of huts on the shoreline at one end of the beach which, she now realized, were most likely all that was left of a Maori village. And higher on the slopes of the hills, the terraces on the sunny northern slopes must have been where kumara had been planted. She felt a fizz of excitement in her gut and knew it was back—that fascination she had with the past.

After having found the few implements she needed from the garden shed, she returned to the beach and began to dig, all the while trying to figure out how her passion had snuck back into her life. She hadn't felt it since she'd met Jonny. At first, her infatuation for him had consumed her love for her work, and at the end, there had been no room in her life for anything but grief. No, she reflected, it wasn't that the sorrow had diminished; she was simply doing what she always did when challenged emotionally—returning to the comfort of the past. The past was played out, gone, and therefore able to be ordered, unlike the present.

Her focus was so complete that she wasn't aware she wasn't alone anymore. Then a shadow passed over the jumble of finds she was examining, and she turned to see the sun obscured by someone standing beside her.

"Hello," said Gabe. "You look busy."

She looked down at the pile of things around her and stood up, wiping her wet, sandy hands on her shorts. "Yeah," she said, pushing her hair out of her eyes. "I guess I got carried away."

"What is it you have there?" He narrowed his eyes at the object she was holding.

"Oh, this?" She screwed up her forehead. "I haven't cleaned it up yet, but it looks like the remains of an old clay smoking pipe." She held it out to him. "What do you reckon?"

He took it and turned it around, rubbing his thumb to reveal more of the carving on the small round object. "Yes, you're right. I found a few over the years. Particularly at Belendroit. I reckon there's enough history there to keep a university going for years."

"Really? Then why hasn't it been excavated?"

"In a word—Dad. He had some argument with the Chancellor at the university and refused to give them access."

"That's a shame."

Gabe shrugged. "That's Dad for you. He loves drama. And if there isn't any, he'll make some."

"You don't seem like that."

"I'm *nothing* like that. I'm more of your 'sitting around a table, chatting, laughing, and having a sociable drink' kind of guy. Want to join me?"

She hesitated. She liked Gabe. The past few weeks had made her like him even more—her guilt increasing in equal proportion. And she knew that, despite what she'd said, his interest was more than platonic. It wasn't in what he said, but what he didn't say. And it was impossible to ignore. She didn't want to lead him into thinking there was any future. And yet, wasn't he the reason she was here? "I was going to go out with Flo."

"Oh, she's coming." He looked around. "In fact, here she is now."

"Right," she said, trying hard to hide how relieved she felt. Relieved and excited too, because it meant she could enjoy Gabe's company without fear.

Once inside the pub, a couple of Gabe's friends joined them. Conversation flowed as effortlessly as the beer and wine and the hours slipped past.

As Flo and Maddy watched Gabe rise and make his way across the crowded room to the bar, Flo nudged Maddy. "He hasn't taken his eyes off you all evening."

She frowned. "We've been talking, yes, but hardly exclusively."

Flo raised a knowing brow. "If you say so."

They both looked over to the bar just in time to see Gabe catch Maddy's eye, grin and turn away.

Flo flicked Maddy's thigh beneath the table. "See!"

"I don't see anything except a friend."

Flo shrugged. "A friend? I wish *I* had that kind of friend."

Maddy was curious. "When was the last time you went out with someone?"

Flo suddenly lost her teasing look. "I don't know. Ages ago."

Suddenly Maddy was curious. "Who was he?"

Flo mumbled something as she ate a mouthful of crisps.

Maddy leaned in, concentrating as she tried to hear. "Who? What was his name?"

Flo repeated the name just as there was a loud burst of music from a band about to start. Flo rolled her eyes. "Rob!" Unfortunately for Flo, the music stopped as suddenly as it started and everyone turned around to look at Flo who disappeared under a flush of bright red.

"Rob?" asked Gabe, placing the drinks on the table. "Are you talking about our Rob?"

Maddy looked from Gabe to Flo. "Are we?"

Flo nodded, the embarrassed flush not disappearing. "I was telling Maddy about your family."

Maddy was genuinely confused. "No, you weren't. You were telling me about the men you—" She paused, suddenly realizing Flo was trying to hide something. "Oh!" She looked at Gabe who frowned.

An awkward silence fell, unrelieved by the band who'd decided to take a break.

"Sorry," mumbled Maddy. "I got the wrong end of the stick."

Flo glanced warily at Gabe who sighed. "I *do* know about you and Rob, Flo."

Flo blushed. "There's not a lot to know. Just a few dates…" She waved her arm airily. "I can hardly remember."

Another silence fell while Flo kept glancing at Gabe who was oblivious to her curiosity.

"How do you know?" Flo eventually asked.

"What?" Gabe glanced at Flo, before taking a drink of his beer.

She took a deep breath. "How do you know about Rob

and me? Not that there is anything to know. Hardly anything at all."

"He told me," said Gabe.

"And *what* exactly did he tell you?"

Gabe looked at Flo with kind eyes. "Do you really want me to tell you here?"

Flo swallowed. "No."

"Okay, then, I'll tell you later. Now, there weren't any more salt and vinegar chippies so I got plain. Hope that's okay with everyone. And some chocolate for you, Maddy." He grinned.

It was like the wind had been knocked out of Flo's sails, and it wasn't long before she made her excuses and left the pub alone, but not before Gabe had had a few private words with her.

"I feel terrible," said Maddy, pulling on her jacket as she and Gabe prepared to leave the pub.

"Why?" he asked.

"For bringing up Rob. She was obviously trying to keep it quiet."

"Don't worry about it." He opened the door and they walked out into an empty street and a warm summer night.

"Poor Flo. She was so embarrassed, and it was my fault. I put my foot in it in front of you."

"Flo will know you didn't mean to."

"Yeah, I guess. Doesn't make me feel any better though. Tell me if it's none of my business, but what exactly did Rob tell you about Flo?"

"He told me that he loved her, but that she didn't love him."

"Wow! What did Flo say?"

"Nothing. She walked away pretty quick. She seemed a bit upset."

"Would Rob mind you telling her that? Come to think of it, why didn't *he* tell her that?"

"In answer to your first question, Rob hasn't been home in years. He's too busy making money on foreign exchanges, or whatever financial people do. And secondly, he's the proudest man I know. And the most secretive. He rarely tells anyone anything. I think he only told me because he knew I wouldn't be that interested and wouldn't spread it about." He shrugged. "I guess everyone has to tell someone the things which are important to them. Which leads me to a change of subject."

He stopped beside a lamppost. A rare bat swooped above them, hungry for insects attracted by the light. She jumped and he reached out to steady her. But he didn't lift his hand from hers, and somehow she didn't move away. He caressed her wrist.

How could such a simple gesture stop every function of her brain except that which focused on the trail of his fingers over her skin? She had no idea, but it did. The bloom of awareness spread from his fingertips to every part of her body. It was like spring touching a bulb after a deadly winter. Heat pulsed at her core, awakening her to life.

She placed her hand over his, and he began to draw away, but she gripped it tighter, holding it in place.

"Gabe," she whispered, half in despair, half in desire. The only thing she knew for sure was that she didn't want him to move away from her. He must have understood because he raised his other hand to hers, and turned to face her fully.

"Madeleine."

She opened her mouth, but only a sigh emerged. A sigh which was cut short by his lips on hers, in the slightest and yet most devastating of kisses.

When he drew back, she pressed her fingers to her lips as if unable to believe what had just happened.

"Um. I knew you'd taste good," he said. "Sort of a mix of moonlight and chocolate."

She laughed, relieved to have the atmosphere lightened. "That's an unusual combination."

"You're an unusual girl."

He hooked his finger around the collar of her shirt and brought her to him once more. She should have minded. She *really* should have minded, but her body betrayed her once more, and all she could think of was how good he smelled and tasted, and how her mouth opened, ready for another kiss.

His lips curved into a brief smile as they recognized the signal and obliged. This time the kiss was anything but brief, and affected all of Maddy's body, sending shivers of desire coursing through every fiber, every vein, bringing it to life, heating the pit of her stomach and turning her insides liquid. When he pulled away, he had to support her as she melted against him. She felt his groan vibrate against her breasts, further stirring her need.

"Hey! You two, get a room!" There was a peal of laughter as Gabe's friends walked by.

Gabe made some comment before turning back to Maddy, who'd stepped away as a cold wash of reality drenched her body and extinguished her desire.

"You okay?" Gabe asked.

She shook her head and pulled her hands from his. Her body was still reeling, but her mind was reeling more from the ice-cold effect of his friend's comment. "I'm sorry, I shouldn't have done that."

"Why not?"

"It doesn't feel right, not so soon after..." She paused and gulped down a breath of sweet, salty air. It was time to tell him a little of the truth. "A close friend of mine died a year ago."

"Oh," breathed Gabe, as if finally understanding something. "I see. I'm so sorry. That must have been painful."

She swallowed and nodded, not trusting herself to speak.

"And how are you doing?" he asked.

"It's been difficult, but I'm getting there."

"Good."

"But, it feels too soon to, you know…"

"Kiss? Date?"

"Both."

"Right." He glanced away, bit his lip and nodded, too vigorously, before turning to her with a smile that was ever so slightly forced. "Coffee?"

"Yes." She exhaled roughly, not having realized she was holding her breath. "Please."

It was a short walk to Gabe's house. Maddy followed him through to the kitchen and stood uncertainly as he made coffee.

They both began talking at once. They grinned at each other. "You go first," said Gabe.

She shook her head. "I was only going to talk about the accounts."

He pulled a face.

"What were *you* going to say?" she asked.

"I was going to say that you looked comfortable out on the beach this afternoon, digging around. You looked more relaxed than I've seen you before." He splashed some milk into his coffee and brought the cups to the table.

"I was. I've always found it absorbing work. It's what I've been doing for as long as I can remember. Anyway, you don't want to hear about that." She took a sip of her coffee. "What do you do to relax?"

"Me?" He sat back and slid an arm along the back of the sofa. She shouldn't, but she couldn't help admiring him, as he talked about his sports and hobbies. He was handsome, confident in a different way to the way Jonny had been, and macho in his own way.

He paused, waiting for a response. She realized she'd stopped listening to him. He leaned forward and took her hand. "You're miles away. You haven't heard a word I've said, have you?"

She bit her lip and shook her head.

He pushed her hair back from her face. "I wish you'd open up to me. Tell me what you're thinking."

She shrugged. "I'm not like you. I'm not used to sharing my innermost feelings."

"Maddy, believe me, I don't."

"But you, you're always..." She trailed off, suddenly aware that the conversation was getting deeper than she'd intended.

"But I'm always surrounded by people? Just because people live social lives doesn't mean they don't keep parts of themselves safely hidden."

She suddenly realized that, despite all evidence to the contrary, Gabriel Connelly kept a part of himself hidden from full view. That was why he was comfortable sharing the public part. Only a very confident person could do that. Jonny had never been able to. Nor her.

She frowned. "You've been hurt."

He drew back from her. "Of course. Hasn't everyone?"

"I guess." She wanted to know who'd hurt him, but she had a feeling she knew already. And she couldn't ask. She stood up instead. "I should leave."

He rose and watched her wordlessly as she gathered her bag and jacket. Finally, she couldn't put off looking him in the eye. And what she saw there made her stop dead in her tracks. Gone was the kind, public persona of the doctor. In front of her was a man with a steely depth in his eyes, and a desire which shot straight to her gut, and lower. She gasped in a quick breath, wondering if he was going to kiss her again. He stepped forward, and she held that quickly gasped breath. He was so close she could smell his outdoor smell, the faintest trace of aftershave, a suggestion of whiskey. It made her knees weak. She licked her lips.

"I know you're still grieving. I understand that, but I think you need a friend. Someone to listen to you, someone to look out for you, to care about you. I'd like to be that friend—if you'll let me."

She had the urge both to run away, and into his arms, at the same time. For a long moment she wasn't sure which urge would prevail. In the end each one counterbalanced the other and she stayed put. "There's no point, Gabe, I won't be here long."

"I can be your friend for as long as you're here. How about that?"

She shrugged. "I'm not… I'm not sure."

He reached out and took her hand, and the warmth and firmness of his grip sent shivers of desire coursing through her. "I'm here for you when you know. Okay?"

She nodded, not daring to speak in case words emerged which revealed the truth—that she knew she wanted him to be more than a friend to her. Because she knew that, if she did, she'd regret it bitterly later. This wasn't just anyone; this was her dead fiancé's brother, his *twin* brother, the man who Jonny had asked her to visit, asked her at the end of six months to give him something, asked her not to say a word before that time. But he was so close. A shiver of pure desire snaked down her back.

Then he pulled away and the intimate moment passed. "Tell me when you know," he repeated. "There's no rush."

She gripped her handbag nervously, and stepped toward the door which he opened for her. "Gabe…"

"Yes?" he asked.

She swallowed. "I'm sorry."

He frowned. "About what?"

Her heart thudded heavily, keeping time to the grandfather clock in the hall. She licked her suddenly dry lips. How could she tell him she was sorry about everything? About the hurt Jonny had inflicted and, not least, that she couldn't do what her body desperately wanted her to do, which was to accept both his friendship and his kisses. She pressed her lips together and shook her head. No, she couldn't tell him anything; she'd promised otherwise. She shook her head again, gave a brief smile and stepped outside into the night.

MADDY DISAPPEARED into the night before Gabe could offer to walk her home. He sighed as he closed the door. She was one confusing woman. Why the hell was he always drawn to people like Maddy? People with a past they didn't want to disclose, people who kept you guessing?

He sank down onto the chair and took another sip of his coffee which had gone cold. Who was he trying to kid when he said people? Mysterious people had always piqued his interest, but not to this extent. Not like Maddy. This was nothing about mystery and all about Maddy.

5

After the night of the kiss—her life was now divided into Before Kiss and After Kiss—Gabe had changed the time she came to work at his house to four in the afternoon. He'd said it was usually quieter around then. But she had her doubts. His surgery was never quiet until after five. And, when she was packing up, he'd always appear, and they'd go for a drink, or a coffee, or sit outside and chat. But over the following weeks, their interactions changed. It was as if he was quietly courting her. There was no overt flirtation but the intimacy of that night didn't disappear and she was aware of a deepening in their relationship. She did her best to keep up her guard, but Gabe was adept at side-stepping it when she least expected it, and stirring her emotions in a way that she didn't want them to be stirred—afterwards, that is, when her brain had returned to functioning mode rather than 'is he going to kiss me,' melting mode.

And each assault on her senses brought him closer to her, breaching the barrier she'd created to keep herself safe. She knew it and, judging by his increased confidence, he knew it.

As Gabe emerged from his surgery, his sensual smile

staked a claim at the farthest most point he'd reached, definitely inside her barrier.

He went to the kitchen sink and ran a glass of water, took a sip and leaned against the bench, as he turned his gaze to her. A shiver of desire ran through her.

"I'm going fishing at the weekend. Would you like to come along?"

She took a calming breath. There he was again, challenging her with his expression, reassuring her with his words. She wondered if he was going alone, but couldn't think of an easy way to ask. "Will there be room for me?" she asked innocently.

He drained his glass and placed it in the sink. "Yes."

She twisted her mouth as she tried not to smile. He knew why she was hesitating. "What do you fish for?" she asked.

"Whatever's there. To be honest, sometimes I never bother to get out the rods, it's just nice to be out on the water."

"On your own?" she ventured.

"No."

"Oh. Okay." She made up her mind. "That'll be great. It's ages since I've been out on a boat."

"Cool. Come to the marina when you've finished at the hostel."

"Shall I bring a picnic?"

"Sure."

"How many people will be there?"

"Just us."

"But you said you weren't alone."

"I'm never alone. There are dolphins everywhere."

She groaned. "You did that on purpose."

"*That* is something I can neither confirm nor deny."

She shook her head, frustrated by his charm and by the fact that she didn't mind.

"Don't tell me it concerns you, being alone with me?" he asked.

"No, of course not." It shouldn't, but it did.

"I wonder why I don't believe you?"

She couldn't admit it. It was ridiculous. They were adults; she enjoyed his company. Trouble was, she wished she didn't. Most of the time she could kid herself, and she could forget that he was Jonny's twin brother. Especially when she was with him because he looked nothing like Jonny, who was dark and lean, compared to Gabe who more closely resembled a surfer than a doctor. Gabe's sunny personality was also different to Jonny's, who could swing between extremes of mood. The highs had made him exciting to be with, but the lows could be bad. And no doubt it was one of those lows, one which had created too much bitterness to be overcome, which had cost him his relationship with his family.

"You know," he continued, "that I like you. I *really* like you, Maddy. But I'm not about to jeopardize our friendship by doing something stupid. You do know that, don't you?"

"Yes, of course." She couldn't ever imagine Gabe acting in any way inappropriate with a woman, despite the glimpses of sexy intensity which he subjected her to when she least expected it. He was too respectful and kind.

He looked at her intently with eyes that made her feel like an open book—which she definitely wasn't for anyone else, even Jonny. "In which case, it must be yourself you're worried about."

She blinked and looked away. He'd hit the nail on the head. She *didn't* trust herself with him. She rose. "I'd best get off. I need to shop for tomorrow and finish off some paperwork at the hostel."

He didn't say anything, but she could see he was satisfied he'd hit a raw nerve. "Sure."

"Bye then." She walked away. At the corner she glanced around to see him still standing there, looking at her.

He might not ever act in an inappropriate way, but she had a feeling that Gabe might think about it.

FLO TOOK a swig of her beer and reached out to deadhead a rose with the other hand. "So tell me again why you're concerned about being alone with Gabe."

"It's not that I'm concerned as such. It's just that... oh, I don't know."

Flo tossed the withered head of the rose to one side and sat back and looked with her usual directness at Maddy. "If you don't, I reckon everyone else does."

"Then why did you ask?"

"Because you're in denial and I thought my question might prompt you to think about it."

Maddy shrugged. Over the weeks she and Flo had slipped into a comfortable friendship. They were very different people but it was easy to respect the opposite when you didn't much like yourself. But even though they were fast developing the kind of friendship which would last distances and time, Maddy really didn't want to get into what her issues were with Gabe.

"He's my friend, that's all there is to it. And I'll go out with him on the boat, and we'll have a fun afternoon."

Flo grunted a swift laugh and rose. "That's all hunky dory, then. I'll leave you to your fantasies. Which, I might say, are the opposite of every other woman who has ever come across Gabe Connelly."

Maddy didn't reply as Flo went inside the hostel to prepare for incoming visitors. Instead, her mind went not to Gabe, but Jonny.

She'd fallen for Jonny from the moment she'd met him.

He was a hotshot lawyer and the most macho man she'd ever met. He was cocky and confident and had soon swept her into his bed. And there she'd stayed. He was as outgoing as she was shy, and he was as assertive as she was diffident. She couldn't believe that he wanted to be with her. He had been separated from his wife and upset about not seeing enough of his young child since his wife had moved to France. But he insisted that with her, he'd found true love. He'd asked Maddy to marry him and had started divorce proceedings with the intention of marrying as soon as they could. Maddy had been swept off her feet emotionally and physically when they took an extended vacation in Thailand. But there, things changed. She'd landed with a bump to find herself uneasy and unsure. By then the first signs of his bipolar illness had revealed themselves. She'd heard of bipolar disorder before but had never known anyone with it. Maybe if Jonny hadn't got mixed up in drugs, and hadn't come off his medication, she'd never have known. But the lows became lower.

She'd hoped that their return to Amsterdam would put him on a firm footing once more, and it had. But it hadn't been easy and there had been times when he hadn't been able to see any hope for the future.

One night, as they'd lain in his apartment in the center of Amsterdam, where he'd lived and worked since he'd left New Zealand, he'd told her about Belendroit, and his family. He'd never spoken of them before. She asked him why he didn't make contact with them. He'd been silent for a long time before answering. His mother was dead, and the argument he'd had with his father had put a barrier between them which he didn't believe could ever be removed. She'd asked him about his brothers and sisters. By his lack of response, she'd gathered that he'd probably equally alienated them. Or, at least, he'd thought he had. The only person he'd mentioned by name was Gabe—his twin brother, whose falling out he'd obviously regretted most. But he did talk about Belendroit and what it had been like growing up there. He'd talked of the sea, the hills, and the town.

In his darkest moments, he'd become intensely emotional, making her promise to return to Belendroit if anything happened to him, to seek out Gabe and return to him a small box. Six months, he'd insisted—no less—to stay and make amends to Gabe. She'd promised—she had no choice, and besides, he was back on his medication, and she hadn't imagined she'd ever have to keep the promise. But she hadn't taken into account the random acts of nature which brought life to a swift close.

In the end, it was no morbid health scare, but a car unable to stop on a rainy, murky night, and Jonny stepping from behind a bus. He'd died shortly after of his injuries.

His family had attended his funeral. Jonny's estranged wife had made all the arrangements, and taken control of his estate immediately. Maddy had stayed away from the funeral at the wife's request. Jonny's child was given as the reason which was enough for Maddy. Besides, she'd said her goodbyes to Jonny. She'd left the next day—run away from everything, but she couldn't outrun her memories, and the fact that she'd made him a promise—a promise she had no choice but to keep.

But why he'd made her make that promise, she had no idea. Was it for some kind of reconciliation with his family which he couldn't effect in person? But, if that were the case, then why didn't he want her to state her relationship with Jonny immediately? He'd insisted that she didn't. Six months, he'd said, during which time she shouldn't make any mention of him. Only at the end of that six months should she give Gabe the object which he'd entrusted her with, and tell him about their relationship. But, then, he'd had no idea that Gabe would stir such unwanted emotions in her, emotions which made her feel like she was betraying Jonny.

Flo, being the fabulous cook she was, had helped Maddy put together a mouth-watering picnic which she'd insisted on packing in a classic wicker picnic hamper. She'd driven Maddy to the wharf where Gabe was sorting out the boat. He waved at them both. Flo stooped to pick up her side of the hamper and whispered: "You're mad. Look at the way that man's looking at you."

"It's just a look. Like you'd give to anyone."

"No, it is not!" Flo smiled at Gabe and spoke between stiff lips. "It's the kind of smile which you give to someone whose clothes you want to rip off."

Maddy caught Gabe's gaze and blushed.

Flo looked at her and shook her head. "You're wasting time, honey."

They walked up the wharf, the green water lapping at the wooden piles from which seaweed clung and floated.

"Morning, Maddy. Flo," greeted Gabe.

"Only just. And isn't it a grand one?" responded Flo.

"Certainly is," said Gabe, looking back to Maddy. "Looks like some picnic you've made there. Here, pass it to me." He hefted it into the bottom of the boat. "Are you joining us, Flo?"

To give him credit, he didn't give any indication that he wouldn't be perfectly happy to have Flo join them.

"No way, Gabe. But thanks for the invite. I've got stuff to do."

"You've always got stuff to do," he responded.

Gabe held out his hand to Maddy, and she took it and jumped on board. The boat rocked, and he held her for a moment longer than was necessary. Flo grinned, waved and walked back along the jetty.

Maddy briefly considered making up some excuse, any excuse, and leave with Flo. But, as if Gabe could read her thoughts, he untied the rope from the jetty and pushed off, leaving her no option but to sit down.

He took up position in the rear of the boat, started the motor and steered carefully out until they were in the middle of the harbor, where he upped the speed, slicing through the cool green water between the two arms of the harbor, heading toward the open sea of the Pacific Ocean.

She could do nothing but sit back and allow the breeze to blow away her fears and doubts and enjoy the ride. The awe-inspiring volcanic cliffs rose up each side of the harbor, from the volcanic crater which formed Akaroa harbor. It was wild, rugged, and utterly beautiful.

It was a twenty minute boat ride to Akaroa Heads. Seabirds swooped and screeched overhead and Gabe pointed out blue penguins on the shore near the ocean, as well as fur seals, as he drove the boat toward the open sea.

ONCE THEY WERE out at sea, a pod of small gray dolphins appeared. They played around the boat, swooping under it, only to pop up and jump out the water. Gabe cut the engine, and the boat bobbed offshore in the gentle swell.

Maddy laughed. "They're so many of them!"

"We have the densest population of Hector's dolphins."

She reached over and splashed the water as one came close to her.

"There are flippers and a snorkel in the cabin if you'd like to get even closer."

Maddy most definitely did like. She often felt too self-conscious to swim on beaches with people sitting around watching her. But, for some reason, she didn't worry now about what Gabe might think of her, how he might perceive her, and she wriggled out of her shorts and t-shirt to reveal her one-piece swimming costume. She put on flippers, a snorkel and mask, and jumped into the water, feet first. She gasped at the shock of the cool water against her hot skin but was soon distracted by the dolphins who swam so close to her.

She heard a splash behind her as Gabe dived into the sea and swam underwater with the dolphins. He surfaced and began to blow bubbles. A small group of three dolphins peeled off from the rest and swam around him as if checking out what he was doing. He started making a funny noise, and yet more dolphins came swooping under, nudging him.

Maddy laughed. "I've never seen anything like it!"

With a flick of their V-shaped tail, they dove into the water, making brief eye contact with her as they went.

"They're curious. Twirl around, make funny noises, and they'll come and check you out."

It was on the tip of her tongue to say that she didn't do that kind of thing. She'd always hated the idea of making a fool of herself—even in only her own company—and would do anything not to. But now she found herself spinning around, not caring how she looked. As the ripples radiated outwards the dolphins responded and swam around her, barely an arm's length away. They were friendly, trusting and much smaller than she'd imagined. They swam gracefully through the water before emerging to reveal their white under-bellies. Then they'd disappear below the green-blue surface, leaving behind a trail of white bubbles.

She continued to play around the dolphins with Gabe, even diving underwater and coming face to face with one before the dolphin followed her up to the surface and swam away. Maddy looked up into the bright sunshine and blinked the seawater away from her eyes, and thought she'd never felt so free. A cold shiver suddenly racked her body, and she realized she must have been in the water a good half-hour, and she twisted to find Gabe watching her from the side of the boat.

She waved and swam over to him. "Hey!" she called, as she grasped the bottom of the step. "Time to get out of the water?"

"Yes, you look cold. But I reckon I could go on watching you all afternoon. You look a different person."

"What do you mean?"

He shrugged. "I mean that you're in the moment. That mask you use to protect you, you left it on the boat."

"Oh!" No one had ever said anything like that to her before. Not even Jonny. Or maybe *especially* not Jonny. His world tended to revolve around himself. Not that she'd realized that at the time. Being with him was like being caught up in a whirlpool, one which you didn't want to leave, not until it was too late and by then you were in too far. "I guess life seems less risky if you can keep your thoughts and feelings tucked safely away out of sight."

"Ah, now, I reckon everyone should risk everything for what they feel in their heart."

"What if people don't know what they feel in their hearts?"

"Then that's a shame. A crying shame. Whatever..." He grunted. "But I hope you don't feel you have to replace the mask too soon."

Gabe reached down to help her back on the boat. Their hands met in a tight clasp as she climbed the steps. He was right. She stood before him now, almost naked, water running off her hair, face, and body, and she felt unmasked. "I hope so, too," she said. She cleared her throat and looked back at the dolphins. "That was amazing," she said as she caught the towel which Gabe tossed to her. "But I guess you're used to it."

"It doesn't matter how many times I do it, I *always* think it's amazing. They're clever, sociable, and we don't know the half about their world. They communicate in all sorts of ways —sonar, pulse. They have over forty types of vocalizations. They have huge brains, they problem solve. It's been proven that they think in abstract terms." He shook his head. "Sometimes I think I missed my vocation. I should have worked with animals rather than people. These dolphins are an endangered species. I'll never take them for granted. "

"True. When you know you don't have something forever, that they might be taken from you, you cherish them."

Gabe stopped toweling his hair. "You're not talking about the dolphins, are you?"

"No."

"Your friend who died?"

"Yes."

Gabe grunted and looked up into the bright sky. When he looked back at her he was wearing his doctor expression—compassionate and kind, but no longer intimate. "I'm sorry. It must have been tough for you."

She opened her mouth to speak but didn't trust herself.

"Do you want to go back?"

His question startled her out of her thoughts. "Back? Where? To Amsterdam?" She shook her head.

He grinned. "I meant back to Akaroa and forgo the picnic on the beach over there?"

She looked where he indicated, across the water to a small cove, farther along the shore. Should she leave all of this? Her promise to Jonny, the fun she was having with Gabe? Should she leave it all and retreat into herself and the past? Suddenly she remembered Jonny's take on her work.

The past? Why bother with it? The future is all there is. She shook her head. "No. I don't want to go back." She glanced at the picnic hamper. "Besides Flo would never forgive me."

"Right." Gabe started the engine. "Good decision. We don't want an angry Flo."

The beach Gabe chose was sheltered by two jutting cliffs, and inaccessible from the land. She set out Gabe's blanket while he brought over the basket. Flo had outdone herself and had included pies as well as a salad, bread, and cheese. Gabe put a bottle of wine to chill in a rock pool, while she opened two bottles of water and sat under the shade of a spare sailcloth he'd strung above them.

He sat carefully at one end of the blanket, and she on the other. Occasionally their arms brushed each other as they reached for something.

"I haven't been out here in years," said Gabe.

"Really? I imagined you came all the time."

"You imagined, eh? And what exactly did you imagine?"

Maddy proceeded to tell him, while keeping a few of her imaginary details quiet, like the fact that he probably always brought his girlfriends here. Looking around, it was the perfect secluded spot for amorous encounters.

"Not far off," Gabe observed. "Not if you replace friends with family. It's here I used to come with my family. My brothers mostly." He raised his eyebrows. "One brother. Before we fell out."

"Which one?" she asked, although she knew.

"Jonny, my twin."

She focused on rummaging in a bag of something so that he wouldn't see her reaction to Jonny's name. When she sat up again he was gazing out to sea, his eyes narrowed against the bright light.

"He was the odd-one-out in our family and the total opposite to me. And we all adored him."

She bit her lip and teased a knot in the cord of her bag with her fingers. She waited for him to continue, but apparently, he needed some encouragement. She cleared her throat. "That sounds odd: so different and yet so adored."

He shrugged. "I think we were in awe of him. Well, the others were. He infuriated Dad, he used to worry the hell out of Mum, my sisters followed him around like the Pied Piper. He was kind of charismatic, you could say." Silence descended again, broken only by the lazy splash and pull of the waves on the shore.

"Go on. Tell me how you felt about him."

"Ah, now that's a long story. Probably without an end because, you could say, it's complicated. He was a part of me, and yet we were highly competitive, and had an intensely volatile relationship. As kids we refused to be apart at night, sleeping in the same bed, but during the day we went our separate ways—Jonny to be with the cool kids, and me to be with the slackers. It was complicated."

"Sounds it." She hesitated but had to know. "So how would you describe him? What was he like?"

"He was intense about everything: he was intensely smart, intense about his feelings, and intensely jealous and competitive. People either hated him or adored him."

"And which did you do?"

"Both. Most of his behavior was explained when he was diagnosed with bipolar disorder."

"And he died overseas, you said?"

Gabe looked up surprised. "Did I?" He pulled a face. "I guess I must have done, or maybe Amber told you."

Maddy tried to cover her faux-pas with a non-committal shrug.

"But, yes, he died in Amsterdam. Got run over by a car. He was living alone at the time. He was separated from his wife and child."

Maddy wanted to scream out that he hadn't been alone, that she'd been with him, waiting for him at home, but she couldn't.

"What..." She cleared her throat. "What did you fall out about?"

"Something stupid." Gabe twisted his mouth with regret before squinting up in the sky. "Something incredibly stupid. I discovered he'd taken something of mine when we were teenagers, something I loved, something which I cherished because it was mine. Jonny being Jonny had always made a fuss about having things first, before passing them on to me. I've always been pretty easygoing, but it got on my nerves as the years went by. I guess Mum humored Jonny because it was easier. The one thing that I'd gotten first, he'd also wanted, especially seeing as how much I wanted it. I think he must have regretted taking it. Not enough to give it back, mind. But enough to wish he hadn't, and enough to lie that he no longer had it. But I discovered it among his things, and it was the last straw. It capped off everything that had been going on for years, and we had a major fight—physical and verbal. My other brothers, Max, Rob and Cameron, also got involved. It was a mess. Jonny took off after that and left no following address. The next thing we heard was from his wife telling us that they'd just got married and had a son on the way, but there was no address, as no doubt Jonny had insisted. And then nothing until a few years later when his wife phoned to say he'd died." He looked at Maddy. "It's terrible, Maddy, when you let arguments drive a wedge between family, especially between brothers."

"Especially between twins," she added. She reached out and took his hand.

He slipped his fingers through hers, grasping her hand, and pulling it to his heart. "I still feel the pain here, in my heart, every day. There's like a yawning gap where something should be. And I don't know how to fill it, or if I ever can. It began when he left, and I know it would have been the same for him. But pride stopped us both from contacting each other. And then the aching emptiness solidified into a mass of aching nothingness after he died."

She spread her fingers over the soft cloth of his shirt that lay between her fingers and his heart—its slow, steady pulse connecting with her fingertips. She looked up into eyes which darkened and held her gaze. "It *will* be filled. The emptiness you feel. I'm sure of it."

He tilted his head to one side, his expression relaxing and the darkness in his eyes, fading. "And how can you be so sure, Lady of the Spreadsheets? Do you know of a magic formula to enter to make a happy ending?"

"There's nothing magic about formulas."

He raised a wry eyebrow. "I can believe it."

"That's because there's no magic required. It's the data that makes the result appear like magic. It's all about the data. That's it."

He rose slowly. "I'll drink to data. The wine should be cold now."

She watched him walk over to the rock pool where he'd placed the wine, and unscrew it as he walked back. She held up the tumblers, and he poured a little wine into each. She rose, and he held up his glass to hers. "Here's to data," he said with a grin. "May I discover what's required to give the correct answer."

They drank but before he could turn around, she spoke. "And here's to Jonny, your twin, the brother you lost but who will always be in your heart."

His eyes shone in the light as they drank to the toast. She picked up the soda water and topped up the wine.

"Good idea," he said. "Half a glass while I'm driving. Even if it is a boat."

. . .

THEY ONLY DRANK a small glass of wine with the soda water, but even so, Maddy could feel its effect on her, relaxing her. And she needed relaxing. She wasn't only keeping a secret from Gabe now. The better she got to know him, the more she felt she was deceiving him. She pushed the thought out of her mind, determined to do what Jonny would have done, and enjoy the moment.

"I feel like Robinson Crusoe must have felt, alone on a desert island."

"Except for his Man Friday." He glanced at her. "Am I your Man Friday?"

"More like Man Saturday," she said, lying back and closing her eyes.

"I could be your Man Sunday and Monday, too, if you like. You only have to say the word."

She opened her eyes to find him seated opposite her, looking at her with a serious expression which he hadn't worn before.

"Gabe, I'm sorry, I can't."

He jumped up and walked to the shore. He threw a pebble, impossibly far, into the sea before glancing back at her as he selected another stone to throw. "Can't? That's a strange word to use. It makes it sound like something's preventing you. And there's nothing stopping you, is there, Maddy?"

He immediately pulled his arm back and threw another pebble so she couldn't see his expression. But she could imagine it from the sound of his voice. There was a barely suppressed yearning that shot straight to her heart. Before she could stop herself, she rose and went and stood beside him. She didn't look at him, she couldn't trust herself. She looked directly out to sea, the bright light making her eyes smart and water. It must have been that. She wiped her eyes with the heel of her hands. When she dropped her hands, she felt his eyes upon her.

"Is there, Maddy?" he repeated.

"I'm sorry, Gabe, but I made a promise which I can't break."

"A promise? That's the first you've mentioned anything about a promise." He frowned. "What kind of promise could stop you from having a relationship with me?"

"I can't tell you."

He grunted. "I suppose that's also part of the promise."

She nodded, not trusting herself to say anything further. She'd always been an honest person and knew that, if he asked a specific question, she was in danger of telling him everything.

"Okay," he said slowly. "So this promise doesn't stop you spending time with me." He paused.

She shook her head. "No." She clipped the word, not wanting to elaborate and tell him that the promise was for the opposite—it required her to spend time with him.

"Well, that's something." He gave her a brief smile. He looked out over the sea toward the lowering sun. "It's time we headed back."

They packed up the picnic things, and Maddy gave one last look at the small beach where she'd heard things about Jonny that she'd never known before. It helped to fit him into family life at Belendroit, and she could now imagine him—charismatic, argumentative and demanding—leading a turbulent life with a family, who, despite everything, continued to love him. She just wished Jonny had known that.

6

Maddy looked back with regret on that day for weeks afterward. Despite her best intentions, she was growing closer and more involved with Gabe with every passing day. She found herself continually thinking about him, trying to figure him out. Gabe spent his life caring for people, and while his family obviously adored him and were protective of him, Maddy couldn't help wondering whether his need to care for people took a toll on him that few could see. Surely you couldn't go on loving and caring for people, without receiving that same intensity of selfless care in return? But, despite her growing obsession, she'd tried to stay away from him because it wasn't fair—on either of them.

She'd been relieved that Gabe had taken her rejection to heart and had done his level best to avoid her. And she'd made it as easy for him as possible, only going to work when she knew he'd be occupied. So when she arrived mid-afternoon, she was surprised to find him at home.

"Hi! No patients?"

"No," he said looking up from his computer with a wary smile. "I'm working on other stuff this afternoon."

"Right. Right." He went back to work, and she took a reluctant step into the hall. "Um, Gabe?"

"Yes," he replied without looking up.

She hesitated but couldn't bring herself to leave. She'd thought of nothing but him and Jonny since their day on the boat, reflecting on what Gabe had and hadn't said, on what his silences had suggested about Jonny's behavior, and its effect on the Connelly family. Jonny had hurt them all badly, and she knew he'd come to regret it. Given time, he'd have made his peace with them, she was sure of it. And when he'd thought he couldn't, he'd made her promise to do it for him. She couldn't leave Gabe hurting. She was sure Jonny wouldn't have wanted her to.

The question was what did she want to do? One thing she knew for sure was that she couldn't carry on in Akaroa without seeing Gabe. She *needed* to see him.

He put down his pen and looked at her. "What is it, Maddy?"

"I… wondered if you'd like to join me in a coffee?"

He tilted his head to one side. "A coffee? Are you sure? It would mean things like"—he shrugged—"conversation. Exchanging pleasantries, even ideas perhaps. Are you up for that?"

"Yes. Definitely."

He raised an eyebrow. "Okay." He rose and held the door open. The smell of his aftershave and freshly laundered shirt was so him. It made her think of things totally unrelated to coffee.

He frowned. "After you."

She hurried into the kitchen and filled the kettle. When she turned around Gabe was leaning against the door, arms crossed, watching her.

"What's up, Maddy?"

"Up?" She plucked two mugs from a shelf and spooned in instant coffee. There was no state-of-the-art coffee machine for Dr. Gabriel Connelly. "Nothing." She looked around in desperation. "I was admiring your home. It's very cool."

He sighed. He obviously knew she was making conversation. "No thanks to me. My brother's an architect."

"Which one?"

"Cameron. He lives in the UK. We don't get to see him often. Just weddings." He hesitated. "And funerals."

Suddenly Maddy remembered a tall, dark-haired, intense man at Jonny's funeral. That must have been him. She'd watched them all from a discreet distance, as Jonny's estranged wife had requested.

"It was Cam who suggested I buy this place. So, you've suddenly become interested in architecture since you've arrived?"

She shrugged and thought quickly. "Flo and I have been looking around her house to see what could be done. It's fantastic but..."

"Needs some investment to make it a going concern? Yeah, I thought that myself. I can always contact Rob and see if he's interested in investing locally. He's done it before. And he has money to burn."

"I'm not sure how Flo would feel about investment, I mean it's her baby."

Gabe shrugged. "It's up to her. If you want to run it by her, I'll do my bit."

She made the coffees and handed him his before sitting down at the table.

He took a sip. "I have a proposition for you."

Her heart really shouldn't have thumped as it did. "A proposition?"

"Don't look so scared. I'm not suggesting anything

improper. I was simply wondering if you'd like to come to dinner at Belendroit tomorrow night."

"Dinner?" she said cautiously. "Just you and me?"

He raised his eyebrows. "We're talking about the Connellys here! No, Dad will be home. And Amber of course."

"Ah, right, that's fine. Thank you."

"And then there's my sister, Lizzi, and her family visiting from Tekapo."

"Ah," she said slightly less enthusiastically. The larger the family gathering, the more she'd feel as if she were being included as a member of that family. She didn't want that, but it was too late now. "Thank you."

"And then Rachel and Zane will be there, of course."

Maddy's heart sank further. She swallowed, wondering how she could back out of it without looking a jerk.

"And then there's Etta. Wherever Rachel goes, Etta will be."

"Who's Etta?" asked Maddy faintly.

"She's Rachel's daughter. And Zane's niece."

"And Rachel and Zane are married?" she asked cautiously.

Gabe waved a dismissive hand. "I know. It's complicated. But that's my family for you. So, how about I pick you up around seven thirty?"

She shook her head, wishing she'd never agreed. From a simple invitation to Belendroit, she'd been cornered into being picked up as if for a date.

"No!" she said, too loudly. She turned around to cover her confusion.

"Oh," Gabe said, sounding disappointed. "You don't want to go?"

She *did* want to go, more than he knew. She'd wanted to see Jonny's home ever since he'd told her about it. "No," she repeated, deciding to pick up on the one thing that made her feel most uncomfortable. "It's not that. I mean I'll make my own way there."

"But it's quite a walk." He frowned. "I'll probably pass you in the car. What's the point in that?"

"The point, Gabe, is that I feel uncomfortable about you picking me up. It feels, it feels, kind of like...."

"Ah," he said. "Like a date." His voice was flat. "You really are against dating me, aren't you?"

She grimaced. "I'm against dating anyone. I'm against anyone looking at us and thinking we're on a date. I'm against feeling disloyal to my ex."

"He's no longer around," Gabe said gently. "Do you believe he'd never want you to date again?"

She bit her lip. "He was very jealous, very protective of me when we were together." She shrugged. "I don't know."

"I can tell you this, for nothing. If he truly loved you, he'd want you to be happy. Okay, that might be on your own, but that might, just might also be with a man. And it's down to you to decide what makes you happy. Don't let it be anyone else's decision. Least of all mine. Okay?"

She nodded. He spoke sense, and she knew it.

"So, are you coming tomorrow?" Gabe asked again.

"Sure."

"Good. A lift?"

She shook her head. "I'll make my own way there. It might seem strange, but I'd prefer it."

"Of course." Gabe stood up and picked up some papers out of the printer. She could tell from his brusque reply and quick movements that he was disappointed that she hadn't taken him up on his offer of a lift. But there was nothing she could do about that. Not yet, anyway. "Now, I'd best get on with my travel arrangements," he continued.

"Travel arrangements? Are you going on holiday?"

He looked at her in surprise. "I'm going back to Papua

New Guinea in a few weeks. Didn't I tell you? I'm a volunteer for *Médecins Sans Frontières*. It'll be about my tenth stint."

"No, you didn't mention it." It was her turn to feel disappointed. And that was even more unreasonable. "Nor did Amber," she couldn't help adding, trying to disguise how out of sorts she felt. By his quizzical glance, she suspected she hadn't done a very good job.

"I guess they're all used to me disappearing, leaving a locum in my place."

Maddy felt suddenly bereft. "How long will you be gone for?"

"Just a month this time. I'm filling in for someone. I'm usually away longer."

"A month," she muttered.

"But of course, if you wouldn't mind continuing with the paperwork, I'd appreciate it. It'll make the locum's work that much easier."

"Sure, no problem."

Two of the six months had already slipped through her fingers. Now another would go without him being here. It should make it easier. Then why did she feel the opposite?

IN THE EARLY evening of mid-summer, the Belendroit homestead lay like a sleeping beauty, drunk from the nectar of the fragrant flowers, and lulled into a half-sleep by the hum of bees and insects and the first chirruping cicadas. Even the trees appeared asleep, unmoving under a cloudless sky. Of the colonial building, only its two chimneys and finials shaped in the form of a windlass emerged from the trees, and only the long veranda—from which hung the lanterns which had given their bay its name—could be seen from the beach path. But there was no one on that path to view the building yet.

Gabe couldn't figure out why Maddy hadn't accepted his offer of a lift. Was he really so unacceptable as a date? He'd never thought about it before. Damn, he'd never had cause to doubt his attractiveness to women before. But now he was beginning to think there was something wrong with him.

He looked around at his sisters and brothers-in-law, seated on the veranda chatting and laughing, none of whom had found love the easy way, but they'd found it nonetheless. And he'd found Maddy who, whether she knew it yet or not, was the one for him.

"Isn't it, Gabe?" repeated Lizzi, as she accepted a drink from Pete, and sat down with the sigh of a busy working mum on the wicker chair. She lifted a Victorian fan which Amber had unearthed from somewhere in the house and began to fan herself.

Gabe turned his back on the view of the beach pathway which wound its way to Akaroa and wondered what his big sister had been talking about. "Isn't it what?"

Lizzi rolled her eyes. "Weirdly hot for this time of year. What is wrong with you? You've hardly paid attention to anything anyone's said."

"Perhaps his mind is elsewhere," suggested Pete, as he poured glasses of wine for everyone. Amber gave Pete a warning glance, but too late because Lizzi had picked up on it.

"Where elsewhere?" demanded Lizzi. "Amber? What's going on? What have you told Pete that you haven't told me?"

"Yes, Amber, what *have* you told Pete?" asked Gabe, with mock sternness. He couldn't be really stern, not with Amber, no one could. Just one glance at her innocent face and you could see there was no malice. No, Amber was an open book. The trouble was she was open with everyone else's books, too.

Amber put down the book on crystals she was reading

and looked at Gabe over the small wire-framed reading spectacles she'd picked up for a song at a thrift shop. With her red hair piled high in a messy bun and her long floaty dress, she looked like someone from a different century. "Just that you've been seen with the mysterious Madeleine around town."

Lizzi gave a low whistle. "Bro! You've been holding out on your big sister. Spill the beans. Who is this mysterious Madeleine; why is she mysterious, and is it serious?" She held up her hand to stop anyone speaking, not that Gabe had any intention of responding. "Don't tell me. If she's mysterious, it *must* be serious, because that's your thing." She sat back and took a sip of wine with a satisfied air.

"Aren't *you* the clever one? If you know so much, why don't you tell me what it is with me and mystery? I'd love to know."

Pete groaned. "Don't get her going, Gabe. You know how much she loves to analyze us all."

Lizzi dismissed Pete's remonstrances with an airy wave. "I'm good at it, that's all."

She fixed Gabe with a focused gaze, and a bright smile, one that Gabe could never resist. Despite her years of heartache with an abusive man, she'd been strong, and she'd brought herself, and her daughter through everything life had thrown at them and had ended up married to the perfect guy—Pete. She could say anything she liked, and Gabe was putty in her hands. But then he was with all the women in his life. Not that he'd let them know. "You think you're good at it, but you don't know what makes me tick." He narrowed his eyes. "I'm an enigma."

"Only to yourself," Lizzi scoffed. "No, you like mystery because you *have* none yourself. *And* you're a sucker for a sob story. You're too kind by half, and want to cure everybody's ills." She turned to Amber, and her bright smile fell. "Don't tell me the mystery woman is hurt, too?"

Amber glanced at Gabe and nodded.

Lizzi groaned. "Oh, shame. But that's it, then. Gabe's gone and fallen in love."

Gabe jumped up and made a dismissive sound. He'd been about to deny it outright, but the words wouldn't come. He strode over to the other end of the veranda and helped himself to some antipasto, trying unsuccessfully to figure out what ingredients had gone into its preparation. He shrugged and shot Lizzi an irritated glance. He liked to be the one who analyzed, the one who cured, not the one who was the subject of so much attention. He held the parcel of unidentifiable food up to his mouth and then thought twice and dropped his hand. "She's just a girl who—"

"You like," prompted Lizzi.

"More than like." Amber grinned.

"Of course I like her. Who wouldn't?" replied Gabe. "She's unpretentious, she's intelligent, she's..." He trailed off, as he tried to find the words to describe just how wonderful Maddy was. But as soon as he'd found a word, he had to reject it again. None of them could accurately describe her.

"She's blonde and gorgeous," said Amber. "And she has legs that go on forever," she added.

Lizzi laughed. "So why dwell on the 'unpretention' and the 'intelligence', Gabe, when it's her beauty which has you hooked?"

He sighed and ate the unidentifiable food. He scrunched his brow. "It's fish. Um. It's tasty."

"Good try at diverting the conversation, but it won't work. And the fish is raw." She grinned as Gabe's expression changed. "Rachel's been experimenting with a New Zealand version of antipasto. It's tasty, isn't it?"

He had to admit it was.

"So?" pressed Lizzi, unwilling to leave the subject, like any self-respecting curious sister. "So, you've fallen for her gorgeousness?"

He helped himself to another mouthful, shrugged and pointed to his mouth. But Lizzi speared him with a glance. She wasn't going to be put off so easily. There would be no getting out of this.

"It's not just her looks, Lizzi. There's far more to her than a pretty face—and figure," he couldn't help adding. "There's far more to her than that."

"Oh," said Lizzi. A silence descended on the small group.

He looked back to the path. "Anyway, you'll be able to judge for yourself any minute. I've invited her to join us."

Suddenly everyone was talking over each other, and jumping up to look down the path, where a lone figure had appeared, still some distance away. Gabe was the only person stationary as two of his sisters, Lizzi and Amber, ran around, adjusting themselves and their surroundings, and Pete followed orders to make sure the wine was in the fridge and to tell their father, Jim Connelly, to come out from the garage where he was mending something.

No one took any notice of Gabe after he'd dropped the bombshell, and he followed the dogs around the corner. Maddy was walking up the path from the beach but hadn't yet seen him. Despite the time they'd spent together, she was still an enigma. She had the looks of a supermodel, the brains of a university professor, and the shy, delicate, untrusting heart of a beaten dog. He didn't understand her, but he would. He never gave up on a beaten dog. He reached down and petted the two cocker spaniels—Stanley and Boo—who were most definitely not beaten, but instead, thoroughly spoiled.

"Come on, you two." He looked up just as Maddy saw him. "Let's go and meet our mysterious guest."

They barked in agreement and trotted happily at his side as he walked down the lawn to where the grass turned into the sandy beach.

He stopped and petted the dogs but didn't take his eyes off her. She looked different and, as she came nearer, he realized why. She was wearing a dress. It was the first time he'd seen her in anything but shorts and a shirt. The dress was neither new nor smart, but its vintage material draped around her long, lean body, and drifted aside with each step she took. And it was covered with flowers. Old-fashioned pink roses with trailing green stems and leaves.

"Maddy," he said, trying, without success, to suppress a grin that he knew his siblings would have described as silly.

She gave him a wary smile. "Gabriel," she said, before giving her attention to the two affectionate dogs who jumped around her, licking her hands and ankles. Gabe understood their impulse. It was all he could do not to press his lips to her uncertain ones, and coax them into certainty. Instead, he thrust his hands into his pockets to ensure he didn't reach out to her, and formed his lips into a smile, rather than a kiss.

"Only my brother, Jonny, used to call me that."

Her wary smile faltered once more, and she glanced away. But when she looked back at him, the smile had returned, firmer than before, as if she'd made a decision. "I like it. It suits you."

They fell into step, the dogs bounding around them. As they turned a corner, Belendroit came into view, and she stopped abruptly.

"What's the matter?" he asked.

She shook her head. "It's just as I'd imagined."

He frowned. "You've imagined this place?"

"Yes."

"What, since I invited you here?"

She shook her head but didn't elaborate. Instead, she bent down and fussed over Boo, who was looking particularly beautiful with her adoring expression, and golden coat gleaming in the late afternoon sun.

He shrugged and decided to take a stab at the answer himself. "I guess it looks intriguing from the Backpackers. What with the lanterns always lit—day and night."

"Why is that?"

"It's an old family tradition which my mother insisted on continuing. Guiding lights for her family's safe return home."

He looked from the house back to her. The expression in her eyes was strange, unreadable, as if she were miles away, looking at him with new eyes. A shiver tracked down his spine. It was as if someone had walked over his grave. Even the two dogs, Stanley and Boo, had picked up on the atmosphere and Stanley, the more sensitive of the two, nudged his head against Maddy's knee as if providing comfort. While Boo, always keen to move on when things became too soppy, found a half-chewed ball and dropped it at Gabe's feet.

Glad of the interruption, Gabe picked up the ball and threw it toward the house. He was off with his aim, and it knocked over a pot, sending the flowers, earth, and terracotta shards everywhere. There were shrieks, a few choice words from his sisters, and a bellowing shout from his father.

Gabe shot Maddy a rueful glance. "Welcome to my family."

He swore and ran up the steps of the veranda where suddenly everyone appeared.

"What are you doing, Gabe?" asked his father, his bushy white eyebrows beetling together.

"Sorry, Dad. My aim was off."

Jim Connelly grunted and bent stiffly to pick up the

pieces. Gabe had a horrible feeling that nothing about this evening was going to plan. "Let me. I'll clear it up. It was my fault."

"It's only a pot!" said Amber, who hated atmospheres of any kind. "I'll tidy it up." She grabbed a shard and dropped it with a sudden squawk, clasping her hand, from which a trail of blood flowed.

Lizzi picked up a tea towel from the table which, unfortunately, had a bottle of red wine on it which overturned and glugged red liquid onto the old floorboards whose patchy white paint wasn't enough to repel the liquid. Pete leaped over and grasped the bottle but not before most of it was lost on the deck. In the middle of it all, the two dogs danced around, spreading the soil from the pot with the red wine and leaping up at Maddy, placing dirty red paw prints all over the delicate silk of her dress.

Gabe grabbed the dogs and steered them away. But by the time he'd returned it didn't look like order had returned in any sense whatsoever. What was with his family? Only Pete was trying to calm everyone by shouting, overly loudly, that there was more wine to be had, as if that would sort everything out.

Gabe turned to look at Maddy, wondering what her reaction to this chaos would be and he was surprised to see she'd stepped away as if preparing to bolt. Her dress was stained red and dirty from the paw prints, but she didn't seem to notice.

"Maddy. Hey, I'm sorry about your dress. Lizzi!" he called. "Do you think we can do something about the stains?"

Lizzi looked up from where she was tending to Amber's cut and grimaced. "The sooner, the better. If you'd like change into something of mine, we can soak your dress."

Maddy took another step back, her face pale as if she'd received a shock. "No, really, it's fine. I'll sort it out at home."

"That might be too late," Lizzi warned. "That silk looks old. It could stain."

"I'll go home now. I was only going to pop in to say 'hello' anyway. So I'd best get back."

"You're not going already, are you?" Gabe asked, while everyone else was focused on trying to tidy up the mess which had erupted so suddenly.

She nodded and stepped away. Gone was any kind of tentative smile, replaced by what looked like distress. "It's for the best."

"Best? Best for whom? Not for me, that's for sure."

"For me, then."

"Look, I'm sorry about the mess. We're not usually so klutzy, honestly. Come and have a drink. Have you got some of your wine there, Pete?"

"Sure." Pete stepped forward and poured a glass for Maddy and held it out to her, saying the first thing that came into his head, to try to put her at her ease. "So, how long have you and Gabe been dating?"

Gabe cringed. "We're not, Pete. Not dating." Unfortunately no one appeared to hear above the dogs' barking. He turned to Maddy. "Stay and have one drink, at least. I promise we'll try to refrain from spilling blood or throwing wine around. Although I can't guarantee that we won't say the wrong thing. *That* is a Connelly specialty. But I can guarantee there will be good food."

Maddy's expression relaxed a little. "Good food is my weakness. Shame I'm a hopeless cook."

"Then I don't know what you're doing dating Gabe," said Rachel with a laugh, emerging from the kitchen. "He can't cook either. You're both going to have to eat out a lot."

Everyone laughed while Gabe shot Maddy, who was looking even more uncomfortable, an apologetic smile. He waited until the laughter had subsided, deciding it would be easier to let the comment pass rather than make a big thing about it.

"You didn't tell me you were dating anyone, mate!" said Zane.

Gabe shot his long-time best friend, and recent brother-in-law, a filthy look.

"Maddy!" shrieked Amber, returning to the veranda after disposing of the remains of the pot, and completely getting the wrong end of the stick. She ran up to Maddy and gave her a big hug. "I'm so happy that you've finally accepted the challenge of dating my big brother. Someone had to!"

Maddy shot Gabe a look, and Gabe knew that this wasn't going to go away on its own.

"We're not dating," he said firmly.

Lizzi, who emerged holding up one of her dresses for Maddy had obviously only caught the word 'dating.' "What's that Gabe?" She turned to Maddy. "So how long have you two been dating?"

His family was beginning to get on his nerves now. "We are not *dating*," he said, emphasizing the word in a way which brooked no further questions. He glared at everyone, daring any of his outspoken siblings to question him further. And his glare, which he rarely gave, obviously did the trick. The mutterings and uncomfortable glances finally came to an end when Zane punched Gabe. "Sure thing, mate. Whatever you say." He turned to Maddy. "Apologies, Maddy. And may I say what extremely good sense you have."

The others laughed, but Gabe noticed Maddy didn't. She looked away as if trying to work out an escape route. He caught her eye and gestured toward the beach. "Fancy a stroll before dinner?"

He'd meant it to be merely a means of escape, but Etta rolled her eyes and made a prolonged "oooo" sound, only silenced when she saw Zane's warning expression. The others obviously thought the same thing but managed to cover it up.

Maddy jumped up. "No, I really should be going." She looked around and not for the first time he was struck by the quiet dignity of the woman. She was beautiful, yes, enigmatic, definitely, but had a gravitas to which his own light-hearted nature was drawn, like choppy waves to a solid rock.

There was a general sense of dismay, overridden by Amber who hugged Maddy. "Of course, there's no chance of a lie-in at the Backpackers. Flo will make sure of that! I'm so glad you came, Maddy."

You could always count on Amber to say the genuine, heartfelt thing, even if it wasn't always said at the right time. But now it was.

Maddy hugged Amber back with genuine warmth. Unbeknownst to him, it appeared his little sister and Maddy had formed a bond behind his back.

Everyone said their farewells, and he followed Maddy around the corner where the wisteria vine practically held up the corner of the house.

Away from the lighted candles and lanterns of the veranda, the lawn was dark, lit only at the end by two solar lamps pointing the way to the beach path. He waited for Maddy to speak but it appeared she wasn't about to break the silence any time soon. He allowed the silence to stretch until they reached the solar lamps and reached out for her arm when she went to continue.

"Maddy, a minute please before you go."

She folded her arms across her waist defensively. He regretted her need to do that.

"I'm sorry if you found my family too much," he continued.

She shrugged. "You have a wonderful family. It's me that's the problem." She paused. "I'm sorry, Gabriel, I should leave."

She backed away. "I should never have come. I thought..." She gulped and looked up into the darkening sky. "I thought I could handle it."

"Handle what?" He opened his hands in disbelief. "My family? Of course you can. They're not usually so crazy." Then he thought again. "On second thoughts, they probably are. But still, they're nothing you can't handle."

"I'm sorry, I have to go."

"At least let me walk you home."

She turned, and her face was pale in the changing light. "No, I'm fine. You go back to your family. I'll see you when you return from overseas."

Without a further word she turned and walked away.

Gabe watched until he couldn't distinguish her outline from the gathering dusk. She'd be fine. The path was safe and rarely used. But it wasn't that which made him reluctant to leave. Her sadness was tangible and all the worse for remaining firmly under wraps. But what could he do? Run after her and force her to tell him her problems? No. He'd helped too many people over the years—patients, friends, and family—not to know how to do it. You had to be consistent, you had to be there for them, you had to listen. But most of all you had to let them approach you. Timing was everything.

Gabe returned to the veranda and met Amber, who was standing by the wisteria looking out across the beach.

"We were too much for her, weren't we?" said Amber, as Gabe climbed up the steps to her. "She wasn't ready for us."

Gabe frowned and looked at his little sister. "What do you mean? How wasn't she ready for us?"

Amber shrugged. "I don't know. All I know is what I see, and that's someone who, behind that calm Scandinavian façade, is quite distressed about something." She shrugged again and turned away.

But Gabe didn't turn away. He stood and watched the path where Maddy had been. She was invisible now. But he refused to blink, refused to take his eyes from where he knew her to be, willing her to turn around, to return to him. But she didn't. Despite how much he wanted her to, she didn't. And there was no sound or shape to fill the emptiness.

He muttered an excuse for Maddy which he knew didn't fool anyone. He took a beer from the table and yanked off the top and took a sip and wiped the foam from his mouth. For once his family had the tact to leave him out of their conversation. So he was left to his thoughts which inevitably led to him staring at the beach, where he'd last seen her. Its emptiness reflected his own. He'd misjudged Maddy. He'd thought she liked him, more than liked. But, even if she did, it wasn't enough to rid herself of the terrors which haunted her, whatever they were. He wished it would put him off her. He wished Lizzi wasn't right. He really, really wished that he hadn't fallen in love with Maddy. He was just thankful that he hadn't given in to his impulses and run right after her, taken her in his arms and kissed her until her heart was mended. Luckily, he was at least in control of his impulses—most of the time.

MADDY WAITED until she'd turned the corner before she allowed herself the release of tears. She'd thought she could do it. Go to Belendroit and meet the Connelly family. She'd imagined it for such a long time that it had become real in her head. But the place was the only thing that was like her imagination. Because in her dreams, in her mind, she'd always been there with Jonny, not Gabe.

All the talk of whether she was dating Gabe had torn at the heart of her. She shouldn't be with him, it was all wrong. When she was well clear of the house, she stumbled from the path down to the sand and fell to her knees behind the shelter of a bush. She doubled over as the pain overwhelmed her at the clash between her visions of herself at the house with her fiancé, and the reality that that man was no longer alive, and, instead, everyone assumed she was Gabe's girlfriend.

It was wrong, *so* wrong. She was in the right place, but with the wrong man. She wasn't with her fiancé, Jonny, but his brother, Gabe, for whom she had no right to harbor such feelings. It was all wrong.

7

Maddy took a deep breath and glanced into Gabe's surgery as she walked past, on the way to his house. There was one person seated in the small front parlor which acted as a waiting room, and Gabe's door was closed. He was busy. She released her breath and opened the door to Gabe's house with the key he'd given her. She walked down to his study.

He'd put the accounts and laptop out for her, which meant he'd still been expecting her. Good. After yesterday, she'd wondered whether he would. She'd certainly been in two minds because she knew that yesterday she'd baffled everyone—including herself. She wanted to be with him, and yet she couldn't be with him. It was as simple and as complex as that. And, as for the rest of the family, they must think she was crazy. It wasn't the impression she'd hoped to give Jonny's family.

Still, she'd come to work. She'd said she would, and there was no point in avoiding him. But she'd work quickly to try to be gone before he emerged. But the minutes turned to hours as Maddy found that the business notes Gabe had left her required more work than she'd first thought. As she worked through the pile of old invoices and ran some statistical analyses on them, she couldn't help wondering why he needed to do such in-depth work before he went away. It was almost as if he were detaining her there. She dismissed the thought as soon as it popped into her mind. Surely not?

She glanced at her watch and hurried through the remaining work. But she evidently didn't work quickly enough, or Gabe worked more quickly, because he'd finished with his patients early and came and joined her in the sunny kitchen.

"Maddy," he acknowledged with a wary smile as he turned his back to her and filled the kettle.

"Gabe," she muttered, wishing she hadn't come. The atmosphere between them was as chill as the southern ocean.

The water gushed into the kettle, and Gabe looked directly out the window at the small tree in the backyard, its uppermost leaves scorched by the hot sun, but still a tender green beneath. It sheltered a small seating area featuring a cluster of bright pink chairs. Amber's work, Maddy assumed. Amber looked out for her big brother, and Maddy remembered all the things Amber and Gabe had done for her since she'd arrived and felt crushed by guilt.

"I'm sorry about yesterday, Gabe." The words tumbled out. She wished her voice was stronger than the hoarse whisper which had emerged.

He half-twisted toward her but not enough to catch her eye. "Are you?" he asked, flicking off the tap and switching on the kettle. He turned to face her, and she almost wished he hadn't. Gone was the affable Gabe, and in his place was a stern man whose thoughts were concealed by eyes which saw everything, but which revealed nothing. She bit her lip, trying to summon up the strength to meet that unwavering gaze.

"Yes, of course I am. It wasn't my intention to turn up and then leave straight away. That's plain weird."

"Yes, that's certainly what my family thought."

She closed her eyes at the impact of his words and looked down at her work. She pushed some papers aside as she imagined the reaction of individual members of the Connelly family. "Yes, I guess they would."

"Of course, if you had a rational explanation, I'm sure they'd reconsider their impression of you."

He paused, waiting for her to explain, but she couldn't. She was bound by a promise that prevented the kind of rational explanation which would make her actions understandable. She looked into his eyes. "It was difficult for a number of reasons which I can't tell you about."

"Secrets," he said, his mouth one firm line. "Of course." His tone was cool and disappointed. He turned his back to her and pulled a couple of mugs from the rack. "Tea? Coffee?"

"No thanks, I'm fine."

He swung around. "And that's where you're wrong. You're not *fine* at all. Something is eating you up." Ignoring what she'd said, he flicked off the kettle before it had had a chance to boil, and poured luke-warm water into two mugs. "There's a whole load of grief inside you which is barely contained by those big blue eyes of yours." He put a couple of spoonfuls of coffee granules into the cups and gave them a desultory stir. They didn't melt but lay bobbing on the gray surface. He looked out across the garden with unfocused eyes. "And until you do, you'll be stuck in 'weird.'"

"I've been stuck there for a while," she said, trying to lighten the atmosphere. It didn't work.

He turned to her again, shook his head, and brought her a cup of the worst-looking coffee she'd ever seen. She looked up into eyes that had no awareness of anything but her. Gone was the coldness, replaced by a heated frustration. "I'm going away tomorrow."

"Oh!" She wasn't surprised that her response sounded as if she'd been punched in the stomach because that was how she felt. She'd become so used to him being around. She couldn't imagine Akaroa without him. "I didn't realize you were going away so soon. I thought you said you were leaving in a few weeks' time."

"Something's come up, so I'm leaving for Papua New Guinea in the morning."

"Wow! That *is* sudden. They were lucky to get you at such short notice."

Gabe's expression made her realize her mistake. The organization hadn't got hold of him, it had been the other way around. He couldn't wait to get away.

"A locum will cover for me while I'm gone." She noticed he didn't respond directly to her comment. She was right. He wanted to be gone from here, and from her, as soon as possible.

She swallowed, suddenly feeling bereft, suddenly aware of how her behavior was affecting him. "Do you want me to continue working here?" Her voice had gotten smaller.

He shrugged. "It's up to you." He held her gaze and drank from his mug, apparently oblivious to its dire taste. "Do you want to continue working here?"

"Yes."

"Why?"

She shrugged. "Because I like it." She licked her lips as she tried to put into words exactly how she felt because she knew that the Gabe standing before her wouldn't accept anything less. "Because I like the work, I like this place...the people. *You*."

He paused. "Do you know what *I'd* like?"

She shook her head, not having a clue what he was about to say. She couldn't predict anything about this new Gabe.

"I'd like you to feel passionate about something. Not just *like*. 'Like' isn't enough for me, and it shouldn't be enough for you."

She suddenly saw the similarity with Jonny, the strength which was on the surface with Jonny, but which lay like a steel spine down the center of Gabe, hidden from the surface, but there, nonetheless.

"I... well, I."

He paced away and thrust his fingers through his hair before twisting round to face her. "Stop it, Maddy, just stop it. You need to sort yourself out."

"Sort myself out?" she replied faintly, unprepared for this lecture.

"Yes. And don't repeat it as if you don't understand what I'm talking about."

She bridled under his stern tone. "I understand your meaning, but what I *don't* understand is why you want me to."

He ground his teeth, his expression grim. "Because I *care*, Maddy. Because I *care*." Just in the use of that word, her irritation vanished. "And you should, too," he added.

"Of course I care."

"Not about yourself."

She found it hard to argue with that. "It's difficult."

He sighed and sat down. "Okay, so tell me what's so difficult about going to a friend's house to meet his family. We didn't bite, nor did the dogs—although that's not surprising, they're never aggressive." A glimmer of the Gabe she knew had returned, and a smile briefly lit his face. "Unlike some members of the Connelly family."

"I thought I could," she blurted out.

He frowned. "Could what?"

"Go with you to your family home, but it wasn't right. It didn't feel right—"

"Okay, slow down. Start from the beginning," Gabe said.

"Right. I told you before that I'm not into dating." She sucked in a sudden breath and focused on her hands, fisting them tight to control the tension which threatened to erupt. "You see, I was engaged to be married."

Gabe sat down suddenly. "What?"

"When my fiancé died."

"Ah." Gabe exhaled slowly, the relief easily visible as he registered the past tense. But when he raised his eyes to hers, she saw nothing but sympathy. "Your 'close' friend was your fiancé."

"Yes. And it's been... difficult."

"I'm sure. And you found yourself among family who had put two and two together, and made five and talked about us as if we were a couple. That must have felt very strange."

She nodded, relieved that he'd understood, even if it was only half the story. "More than strange. I felt disloyal." She shook her head vehemently as she recalled her feelings. "And I felt duplicitous, a liar... so many bad things that trashed the memory of my fiancé and me, of our relationship. But I'm sorry, none of that has anything to do with you, and I shouldn't have gone tearing off like that. You and your family must think I'm crackers."

"No, of course not." After a slight hesitation, he shrugged, as he'd reconsidered. "Well, maybe a little."

She grinned at his honesty. "I'm only strange about that one thing. Honest."

"Just the one? That's far less than most of us."

She laughed. "You're just trying to make me feel better."

"Am I succeeding?"

"Not really. But please apologize to your family."

His eyes narrowed on hers. "No, I won't."

"What?"

"No, I won't apologize. *You* can."

"But… Gabe. Please."

"Ah, you call me Gabe now you want to get around me."

She shook her head and sat back looking troubled. He took pity on her. He leaned forward and took her hands in his.

"*I* won't apologize, because *you* should. Go round to Belendroit, see my dad while I'm away and apologize. Come on, Maddy. It won't mean anything from me. And, if you can pluck up the courage to return to Belendroit, it'll help you to move on."

"But—" Colliding thoughts tied Maddy's tongue.

"But… you don't want to move on?" Gabe asked gently.

She shook her head. Tears threatened, and she pulled her hands from his. She grimaced and squeezed her eyes shut. He sat back in resignation.

"Then why are you here, Maddy? Why are you here in Akaroa, with me now, if you don't want to live your life?"

She opened her eyes and willed her eyes to communicate a small part of her pain and confusion to him. "Because *he* wanted me to live my life," she whispered huskily. "Because I promised *him* I would."

He opened his mouth to speak, but closed it again. Perhaps she'd succeeded. "He must have been some guy," he said quietly.

She nodded. "He was."

"Then you have to do it. Not only for you but for him. Think of it as his last gift to you."

She shifted her mind away from the pain inside. His words threatened to disintegrate the last threads of her control. She knew she'd break down into a quivering mess but she just hoped it would be later, not now, not in front of Gabe. In an effort to rein in her emotions, she looked down into her cup of cold coffee which was looking worse than it did before, if that were possible, and took it to the sink.

"This," she said, swilling the cup under the tap, "must have been the most awful cup of coffee I've ever tasted."

Gabe grinned. "Insult my coffee-making skills if you must, but you can't divert attention away from the fact that you have to get on with your life. You owe it to the both of you."

She turned to face him and gripped the kitchen bench. "You're right, Gabe. I know you're right. I have no choice."

He summoned a weak smile. "It sounds like you're bolstering yourself up. But do whatever you have to do. Sometimes in order to go on, you have to trick yourself. But those first fake steps become a habit, and before you know it, you find you're engaged with life again, that you're enjoying it."

"So... where do I start?"

"Start? How about by telling me about yourself. Not your fiancé, unless you want to, but about yourself."

"Sure." Maddy leaned forward, feeling as if a load had been taken off her shoulders. "What do you want to know?"

"Everything," he said. "All the things you've been holding back from me." Then he went to the fridge and took out a couple of beers, flipped their caps, and offered her one. "I think you'll like this better. I didn't make it."

She grinned. "Thanks."

"Start by telling me why you're doing people's accounts when you're a trained and experienced archaeologist."

"Ah, that." She took a sip of her beer. "I worked for universities for a few years after graduating but gave it away after I met my fiancé. He wanted me with him and my contract had ended at the University of Amsterdam. And after he died? Well, I didn't want to stay in one place." She shrugged and frowned, her mind far away. "So I moved around and adapted my skills."

"And you don't mind doing work like that?"

"No. I know some people are challenged by computers and organizing data, I know it's not everybody's forte, so I'm glad to help."

"And I'm glad of your help. But, you know, the University of Canterbury in Christchurch has an archaeology department. While you're here, why don't you check them out? They organize digs from time to time on the peninsula. Not ancient history, maybe, but still interesting. They research Maori settlements, and early colonial times."

"Oh!" For a moment Maddy's interest was piqued, and she had a vision of herself working on such a project. The vision faded as quickly as it came. "No. I'm only here for six months tops."

"They're not going to worry about that. I bet they'd welcome someone with your specialist expertise."

"Why are you keen for me to do this?"

"I like you, Maddy. I *really* like you. Don't worry, I'm not trying to compete with your fiancé. I hope we're friends, and friends help one another. And I'd like to help you if you'll let me."

She smiled without hesitation. "I'll let you. And thank you. I'd forgotten what it was like to have friends."

"You must have them."

"Of course. But, I've gone off the radar this last year and haven't been in touch."

"Why?"

"I guess I didn't want to be happy, not without… not without my fiancé."

"And now? What's changed?"

Her smile faded, but her gaze became firmer. "I'm keeping my promise to him."

Gabe frowned. "And what was the nature of that promise?"

"All I can say is that part of that promise was to keep it quiet. Not to tell anyone."

"That sounds mysterious."

She shrugged. "It made sense to him. I'm not sure why. But part of it is staying here for at least six months. Which seems pretty hard when you haven't stayed anywhere longer than a few days."

"Why here?"

She shook her head. "I can't say."

"Can't or won't?"

She bit her lip and shook her head again. "I'm sorry, Gabe. I'm just trying to keep my promise. For reasons of his own, he wanted me to stay here for a length of time. He knew I'd find it hard."

"He knew you'd feel lost."

She nodded. "But I wasn't always lost."

"Then maybe you'll be found again. Soon, I hope."

She hoped so too. But no matter how soon it was, she didn't think Gabe would want to be around when the truth emerged.

LATER THAT EVENING, Maddy and Flo were sitting outside drinking tea when Gabe walked up the path.

"Evening, ladies," he said. "Mind if I join you?"

"Join away, doctor," said Flo, rising. "I've work to do anyway. I hear you're flying off again tomorrow."

"Yep, first thing." He pulled something from his back pocket. "I've just come to give you this." He held out a business card to Maddy.

She took it and turned it over. It was from the university. "I got in touch with an old friend of mine at the university who has a mate in the archaeology department. As I mentioned before, they've been keen to carry out some work in Akaroa for some time."

She took the card reluctantly. "Thanks, but I'm not sure."

"What are you not sure about, Maddy?" asked Flo. She took the card from Maddy's hand and turned it round, read it, and handed it back to her. "It sounds like a good opportunity."

She frowned as she looked at it, feeling a familiar fizz of excitement in her gut at the sight of the university crest and motto. She looked up at Gabe who was leaning against the pillar of the veranda. The last rays of sunlight cast a golden light around him, obscuring the detail of his face. But she could feel his eyes searching her for an answer. She felt a rush of warmth for this man who'd gone out of his way to help her. "It's very kind of you. Thanks."

"But..." he said. "I feel a 'but' coming on."

She shrugged. "I don't think I'll contact them." She laid down the business card on the table, but its presence filled the air between them.

"Why not? Surely you can't be fulfilled by doing accounts day in, day out, with some hostel cleaning thrown in for variety." He glanced at Flo. "Sorry Flo, no offense intended."

"None taken." Flo looked at Maddy. "He's got a point, Maddy. This seems like too good an opportunity to miss."

"I'm fine as I am. I don't need anything else."

Gabe sat on the bench facing her. "Now, Miss MacGillivray, I would suggest the opposite and, as you know, I'm a doctor, and you can trust me."

The others laughed.

"Ah, but I'm also a doctor," said Maddy, "so I can also trust my own instincts."

"You're a doctor, Maddy?" asked Flo. "You didn't tell me that!"

"Not of medicine. The Ph.D. was in archaeology."

"Ah, so I rest my case. I'm in a better position to advise on your health," said Gabe.

"Physical health. Not mental, or emotional," she added. "Besides, I don't *want* to do it."

He caught her eye, and she couldn't look away. Flo cleared her throat and rose "I'd best go and clear up."

Neither of them said anything as Flo's footsteps creaked through the house to the back room where they heard her talking to a resident.

He sat forward, his arms resting on his knees, less than a table width between them. "I don't believe you."

She blinked and looked away. She couldn't meet his gaze without admitting that he was right.

"Maddy," he said, tilting his head to one side, so she had no choice but to look at him. "Come on, what's this about?"

"It's about the fact I'm here for six months only—"

"It could be longer if you wanted it to be—"

"And I want to keep things as straightforward as possible."

"Meaning you don't want to enjoy yourself too much, or else you might stay."

She grunted with annoyance. Why was he so determined to make her stay? "No, I won't stay. I *don't* stay anywhere."

"You could start."

She shook her head.

"Not that you're interested at all, but there's a rumor that there was a fort at Belendroit in the early days, you know."

She frowned. "What, like a blockhouse?"

"What's a blockhouse?" he asked.

"It's like a house on huge stilts which people could retreat to if they came under attack. I guess it was the nineteenth-century equivalent of a motte and bailey castle—palisades and earthworks all around to protect it, and ultimately a safe place people could withdraw to. So you think one of those was at Belendroit?"

"So they say. But no one knows for sure because Dad had this argument with the Chancellor at the university—God knows over what—and refused to give permission for a dig which had been in preparation for years."

"That's a shame. Because now I think about it, the setting would have been perfect for a blockhouse. Natural protection all around."

"Yes, it's too good an opportunity to miss. That's what I thought." But by the way he was looking at her, he didn't know if he was referring to unearthing something archaeologically significant on the site or getting Maddy involved. "So that's why I brought it up with Dad again."

She shook her head in disbelief. "You don't waste time, do you?"

"No, there's none to waste."

"So what did your Dad say?"

"I've managed to persuade him that a small dig would be a good idea. I worked on the fact that I know he'd enjoy having the people around. Plus the fact he'd been proved correct in this stupid argument he had with the Chancellor didn't hurt. The university is keen for you to be involved, Maddy." He rubbed his finger thoughtfully against his lips. "I thought you might be interested in the fact that his GIS engineer is on sabbatical at the moment, and they have some expensive equipment lying around without anyone skilled enough to use it."

Before she knew what she was doing her curiosity had gotten the better of her, and she picked up the card again, and read it, her interest piqued despite all the arguments to the contrary. "Really? What kind?"

Gabe grinned. "God knows. You'll have to call him to find out."

Then she realized that Gabe had won. She'd call the person on the card because she was too darn curious not to.

"Well, okay, if it helps them out over the summer, and I'm around, I guess it would be silly not to."

"Crazy. Irresponsible even," he added with a grin.

"Okay, you've made your point." She paused. "Thanks again." She was fully aware that Gabe must have pulled quite a few strings to get this organized.

"No problem." He sat back, and grinned. "So you're going to call him?"

She nodded and smiled, no longer able to suppress her excitement at the thought of returning to the work she loved. "But what about your accounts?"

"You've organized me, you've set up systems to continue to organize me, so I think you can safely say your work with me is done, don't you?"

"I've thought that for some time. But you've kept me on anyway, haven't you?"

He shrugged. "I don't turn away a good thing." And from the look in his eyes, she knew that that comment didn't only include her computer skills. He stood up. "I have to go."

She rose too. "Thanks for everything."

"You don't have to thank me. Just call the university, and keep that promise to your fiancé. Get involved, find your passion again." Without waiting for a response, he turned and walked away.

She watched Gabe disappear around the corner and tapped the card on the arm of her chair. He was right; everything he'd said was correct. She was an intelligent woman who was letting her past destroy her present. For Gabe's sake, as well as for her own, she had to apply the same kind of focus she gave to other people's past, to herself.

And the trouble Gabe had gone to on her behalf made the focus a lot easier. It was like something was pulling her forward into her future, a future of possibility and hope, instead of anchoring her into a past from which there was no escape. With Jonny's firm hold on her memory she felt guilty when she was happy. She felt disloyal when she found she'd forgotten him for a while, and most of all she felt angry—angry that he'd left her. It was stupid, it was irrational, but there it was. Seemed the science nerd wasn't so in control of everything after all.

Yes, she needed to apply her scientific rigor to herself. She imagined herself as an historical figure, someone she was discovering from the past. She held up that person and inspected her, and began making plans—plans composed of straightforward, logical steps. She had work to do to unravel the knots and chaos which her past had wrought, but with Gabe's help, she'd make a start.

8

Maddy marked another discreet black tick on the wall planner in Flo's office cubbyhole and stepped away to survey her handiwork. The seventies anglepoise lamp shone on its laminated surface, illuminating the row of ticks which marked the days since she'd arrived.

Flo had assumed it was Maddy's way of checking off the day's workload. She was partly right. Maddy was checking off the days, but the check mark in the bottom right-hand corner of each day had nothing to do with workload. Maddy was counting down the days until the six months of her promise to Jonny was over. But the calendar before her indicated that only half that time had passed.

"Sorry, Jonny," she said under her breath, before turning away.

She couldn't do it any longer. She thought she could keep up the pretense of being a casual visitor while getting to know Gabe and the rest of the Connelly family for Jonny's sake. But it had all been a whole lot easier before she'd fallen in love with Gabe, before she'd become attached to the whole Connelly family, before she'd felt that Akaroa could be the one home that she'd never dared imagine she could have. But nothing was easy anymore. And she had to face up to that, for Gabe's sake.

She glanced at the clock. Time to go.

MADDY HAD LET a week go by before she'd plucked up the courage to ring Jim Connelly. She had the feeling he'd been expecting her call—no doubt primed by Gabe—because he'd immediately invited her to Belendroit for afternoon tea. And here she was—punctual and very, very nervous. She smoothed down her dress and looked around, unsure of her welcome despite what Gabe had said, despite the invitation.

A light drizzle fell, and Belendroit looked different somehow—less scary, softer and more settled in its environment. She cast a professional eye around, and she could see the signs which shouted its historical significance. She briefly wondered why she hadn't seen them before. But then, as she stepped forward and her heartbeat quickened, she knew. She'd been completely overwhelmed by her emotions on her one and only visit.

But now she could see the tell-tale dips and depressions in the ground; how the vegetation changed according to the pH of the soil, revealing rubbish tips, potentially rich with finds. Not everyone could have seen the signs, but years of experience meant that Maddy could. She suddenly remembered a conversation with Flo when she'd told Flo that Maddy, and others like her, would love Flo's house. Flo's response had been that "People like you don't come along every day." Well, she thought looking around with satisfaction as her brainwave formed into a plan, once this dig took off, people like her would be all around here, looking for somewhere to stay. Somewhere just like Flo's place.

But she'd think about that later. She turned to the house

somewhere inside of which Jim Connelly was waiting for her. The house was hidden from the road by a small copse of trees but, once down the driveway, it revealed itself in all its colonial glory. Old-fashioned and full of character, its two wings embraced a large veranda which was the main living area in summer. Sheltered by a roof, it looked like the contents of the house had migrated outside for the summer. There was an eclectic mix of cushions, shawls, books, teapot, and other objects scattered around the cane chairs and table. A sunshade extended over the area onto the lawn where children's toys were getting wet in the gentle, misty rain. It was the most inviting home she'd ever seen. And yet Jonny hadn't spoken of it until those last few weeks when he'd started to recover.

She heard her name called, and she spun around. Jim Connelly emerged from the corner of the house where a wisteria grew around one of the old lanterns. He waved to her. "Madeleine! How lovely to see you." He had the kind of theatrical voice which carried easily across space. She smiled. Jonny had had the same kind of voice. But not Gabe. He rarely raised his voice; he didn't need to, people always listened when he spoke.

She waved in response but didn't bother to answer until she was closer. She most definitely didn't have that kind of voice either.

"Mr. Connelly!" She extended her hand which he took and raised to his lips and kissed. She laughed.

"Jim, please. What a pleasure to see you, Madeleine."

"Thank you for inviting me. I wasn't sure I'd be welcomed after the way I'd disappeared last time I was here."

He gestured for her to climb the steps to the veranda. He followed alongside. "What can I say, my dear? My family is quite beyond the pale. They're noisy, rude and uncivilized, and you, quite obviously, aren't. I'm not surprised you turned and fled."

He offered her a seat, and she sat down. "You're very kind, but it wasn't your family who was rude, it was me. Please accept my apologies. I didn't intend to be, but I found it... difficult to be here."

"Yes, I hope you don't mind, but Gabe told me a little of your past."

She shrugged. The thought made her feel uncomfortable, but it would also make it easier if she didn't have to explain everything. "Oh, no. That's fine."

"Well, I'm sorry. Bereavements are always difficult, never easy. And it's up to those remaining to find a balance between grieving and remembering our loved ones, and moving on."

She swallowed. She'd expected superficial commiserations but had got something deep and moving instead. But he *was* Gabe's and Jonny's father after all. "Yes. I think that will take me some time to work out."

"There's no hurry. In my experience, it's best to take your time, don't rush it."

She gave a wobbly smile. "Thank you for your understanding."

He grunted. "At my age, it'd be a poor show if I hadn't learned a thing or two." He raised his eyebrows. "Although if you listen to my children, you'd think I didn't know a damn thing. Anyway," he said, gripping the sides of the chair. "Would you care for some refreshment? I do believe Rachel left some iced tea in the fridge. And no doubt other delectable and healthy things to lure me away from the cream buns for which I have a definite weakness."

"Yes, that would be lovely." She'd heard all about Rachel and her culinary expertise. These days you couldn't turn on the TV without seeing her at work inside the Belendroit kitchen.

"Follow me inside, Madeleine. And may I say what a pretty name you have. I wanted to call one of my daughters Madeleine but my wife had an unpopular aunty with the same name." He shook her head. "There was no moving her."

"It would seem aunties have a lot to answer for. Apparently, my mother had an aunt Madeleine who she liked, hence my name. That's what my uncle told me, anyway."

She sat down where Jim indicated, while he peered into the fridge. "Aha!" He withdrew a pitcher of iced tea, complete with fresh mint leaves on top. He set it on the bench while he retrieved a glass. "I have to say, having Rachel back in Akaroa is wonderful. Apart from being a thoroughly lovely woman, she bakes divinely."

"But Amber bakes too, doesn't she?"

Jim peered at her over his glasses. "She does bake, that much is true. Have you tasted anything she's made?"

Maddy shook her head. "No, I think she's always offered me food she hasn't baked."

"She must like you, then," Jim said dryly. "You see, Lizzi and Rachel take after their mother, and are both fantastic cooks, whereas Amber, bless her, takes after me. Our passions lie in other directions. Mine in the theatre, and Amber in her art. Unfortunately Amber hasn't yet quite come to terms with the fact that she can't do everything. She's a dreamer, you see."

"She may be a dreamer, but I think she's wonderful." Maddy felt protective of Amber, feeling that Jim shouldn't be quite so critical about his youngest daughter's skills, or lack of them. "She was the first person to befriend me when I arrived in Akaroa. She gave me food, coffee, found me a job and a place to stay, all within half an hour. I don't know where I'd be without Amber."

Jim smiled. "Nor me. She's my baby, and I adore her. Even if she can't cook," he added, passing a plate heaped with biscuits to Maddy. "Now, take a seat while I put this coffee machine on which Rachel insisted on installing. I have a feeling she prepared the iced tea for you; coffee is more my thing. I'm not sure I've got the hang of this machine yet."

Maddy spent a pleasant hour talking with Jim about anything and everything, including the possibility of doing some archaeology on his land. He was surprisingly amenable, with no mention of any ill-feeling toward the university. It appeared Jim could forget an argument as easily as he created one.

It wasn't until she rose to leave that Jim put his hand on her shoulder and spoke the words which made her heart stop.

"I do know."

She frowned, immediately thinking the worst. But how could he? "Sorry?"

"I do know your secret. I thought you might say something, but as you haven't, I will. I know you were Jonny's fiancée."

She gave a small cry, a blend of dismay and embarrassment. "But…"

"How? Because, my dear, your name kept cropping up. MacGillivray. A Dr. M. MacGillivray was mentioned in Jonny's will, which I was the only member of the family to see. Dr. MacGillivray's address was care of the archaeology department in Amsterdam. Neither Gabe nor Amber mentioned your surname when they spoke of you but, when the archaeology department in Christchurch contacted me, they mentioned a Dr. Madeleine MacGillivray and I did a bit of research. I found your old staff photo still online at Amsterdam University. And when I saw you the other day, the pieces of the puzzle slotted together. He sent you here, didn't he?"

She felt sick with shock, and nodded, mutely. Of all the ways that she'd imagined revealing this information, this hadn't come close to being one of the possibilities.

"I'd like to hear as much about Jonny as I can. We missed the last few years of his life, and it hurts still. But you don't have to say anything until you are ready. All I ask is that you don't disappear without coming to me, at least to me, and talking to me about him."

She nodded. "Of course. I was going to, except not yet. I promised Jonny I wouldn't say anything for six months."

"Ah…he put a time limit on it, did he? A period when you could get to know us, and us you, without the added complication of his presence." He was silent as he thought. "His last gift, I think."

"I think so. I think he wanted me to fill you in on his life. He left me some things to give to you and Gabe, but made me promise I'd wait six months."

Jim nodded. "A gift for everyone, maybe."

She frowned, not quite understanding his meaning but he moved on swiftly. "A promise to Jonny or no, I think maybe it would be kind to tell Gabe sooner rather than later. Before he falls completely in love with you."

She licked her lips of her suddenly dry mouth. "What?" But even as she said the word, she knew he was right. It was more than a friendship, a lot more. She just hadn't wanted to acknowledge that fact.

"Promise or no promise, Gabe deserves to know the truth," repeated Jim.

"Yes, of course he does. Everyone does," she said, trying to widen the focus away from Gabe. "But, if you wouldn't mind, I'll tell Gabe in my own time."

"Of course. But don't leave it too late."

"I won't. I'll tell him as soon as he returns."

"Good."

They walked together in silence down the steps, both lost in their thoughts, of the past and the present, and maybe the future.

"Goodbye then. And I look forward to talking more when you're ready," he said.

"I'll call you. Thanks for everything."

Jim waved and turned away quickly. Maddy suddenly realized how much her and Jonny's actions were impacting not just on them, but the whole family. If Jonny were alive now, would he want her to continue this charade? No, she thought, as she walked toward the beach path. No, he wouldn't. Jonny might have let his own needs drive his life, he might have been strong-willed and unforgiving sometimes, but he'd never been unkind; and he'd never lost his deep love for his family, no matter what they might think. She stepped off the lawn and onto the beach path. And it was up to her to show the Connelly family how much Jonny had loved them all. Starting with Gabe.

~

MADDY WAVED goodbye to the locum and stepped out of Gabe's house into the sunshine. It felt far longer than a month since Gabe had left. Partly because she'd done such a lot, met so many people, and completely immersed herself in her new life, and partly because she'd missed him.

Since he'd been gone, she'd found herself looking around when someone called her name, a smile forming on her lips, as she sought his face. But of course, it hadn't been him. It had been the locum, or one of the archaeology team she'd been working with since they'd begun work at Belendroit. Gabe hadn't exaggerated how keen the archaeology department was to work on the Belendroit estate, or to have her involved.

And when Jim Connelly had given the green light, the university had wasted no time in getting to work. Which meant she and Flo hadn't had a minute to themselves as they prepared the house to accommodate the archaeology team, because much to Flo's surprise, the university had approved Maddy's plan—the team was to stay at Flo's place for the duration of the dig.

Between the house, the archaeology, the university, and keeping up with Flo's and Gabe's accounts—which Maddy was determined to do—her days were full, which was fine by her.

But at night when all the people and busyness had faded from her life, and all she could hear was the muted splash of the sea on the beach outside her window, thoughts of Gabe, and of Jonny, filled her mind.

Jonny had forced her into this situation, and she'd accepted the promise and gone ahead, knowing that he intended to heal his relationship with Gabe. But why six months? And why incognito? She didn't know. But the experience had proved to be very different to how she'd imagined it to be. She'd thought she'd go through the motions, exist on a superficial day-to-day level. But the reality had been that she'd been forced to participate, to make connections with people and things, which once lodged, refused to shift. She visualized herself as Gulliver tied to the earth with myriad thin strands which she'd awoken one morning to discover. It had happened slowly, imperceptibly, without her noticing. Otherwise she might have bolted. She just hoped she'd be strong enough at the end of her allotted time to uproot the invisible ties—that they weren't rammed in too deep.

And one of the strongest ties was to Amber, who she was on her way to meet. They'd fallen into a habit of meeting every day after she'd finished work. They'd hang out on the beachfront, share a chat, and some café leftovers. Sometimes Maddy would go back to Amber's small cottage and view her latest artwork. It was often hard to know how to comment because Maddy wasn't particularly arty, and Amber's work wasn't particularly accessible. But, as Maddy approached their usual picnic spot, she didn't see the familiar sight of Amber's red hair and bright clothes. Instead, there was a man looking out to sea, with his back to her. She stopped walking abruptly, her heart skipping a beat. It couldn't be. Surely she'd have heard if he was back? Then he turned around, and a warm smile welcomed her.

"Gabe!" she mouthed. No sound emerged. It was as if all the air had left her body. There was a gap of a dozen steps between them, which he made no effort to bridge. It was up to her. She walked toward him on legs which seemed to have forgotten how to function.

"Gabe," she said again, stronger now.

His eyes roamed over her. "Maddy! It's good to see you."

She nodded. "And you."

"Amber told me you'd be here," he said.

"Ah, I wondered why she was a no-show."

"Fancy a walk?" Gabe asked.

For several seconds neither of them spoke. There was simply too much to say.

"Sure."

He gestured toward the beach path, and they fell into step.

"How have you been?" he asked.

"Fine. Keeping busy."

They both grinned and looked away at the same time, reverting to the conversation of strangers while their glances and tone of their voices revealed the opposite.

"And how about you? Was it hard in PNG?"

"No more than usual. We've been working to improve access to treatment for TB. It's rife over there. I was working with local doctors out in the community. It's humbling stuff." He stopped walking and turned to her. "What's happened here?" He cocked his head to one side in a pretense at studying her features. "You look different somehow."

"Do I?" She shrugged, but she knew deep down that Gabe was right.

"Yes. You've caught the sun on your face and your eyes look brighter. You look happy. If that's what happens every time I go away, maybe I shouldn't see you again?"

It was meant to be light-hearted, but Maddy could feel the seriousness underlying the question. Time to begin to tell the truth. She shook her head. "I've caught the sun because I've been working outside on the dig. And my eyes? Well, if they're bright it's not because you went away, it's because you're back. I guess I'm happy to see you again."

A self-satisfied smile spread across Gabe's face. "Good. Then maybe we should see a bit more of each other now I'm back. What do you think?"

"I think..."

"Yes?"

"I think we need to talk first."

"That sounds serious."

"Yes, it is."

"We can talk now if you like."

"I'd prefer to talk at Belendroit."

"You want to talk to me at Belendroit? Why?"

"Because then I can also show you around. Would you like to come to dinner?" She grinned at the look of disbelief on his face.

He frowned. "Let's get this straight. You're inviting me to my family home for dinner?"

"That's about the sum of it."

They stopped outside the Backpackers. The drone of a vacuum cleaner drifted out to them through the open windows. "We had a load of people leave today." She paused. "Which means cleaning. I'd best go and help Flo."

"Sure. So I'll see you later, then?"

"Uh-huh. Around seven?"

"Sounds good."

She resisted the urge to touch him and walked quickly into the house and shut the door, her heart beating fast and her face flushed. Flo looked up and stood with hands on hips and a big grin on her face. "I take it you've seen Gabe, then?"

Maddy shrugged but couldn't contain a smile. "I don't know what makes you think that."

Flo rolled her eyes. "Because you look like someone's lit a flame inside you. That's all." Before Maddy could respond Flo offered her the vacuum cleaner. "You may as well use some of that pent-up energy here."

Maddy took the vacuum hose from her and Flo walked off laughing. "You've so got it bad!"

As it happened, Jim had invited Maddy to dinner at Belendroit that evening to meet Rachel, who'd been in the US with her family exploring sports scholarships for her daughter. They'd returned a week before, and Maddy knew that the Connelly family considered the only thing better than a family gathering was a big family gathering.

As Maddy emerged from the path onto the beach, she turned at the sound of voices. At the end of the jetty were two girls. The older one was trying to teach the younger one to fish. She paused to greet them, but neither turned around.

"Aimee!" said the older of the two. "Stop wiggling it around and hold it still. You'll never catch anything like that."

"I don't want to catch anything. Think of the poor fish."

"Poor fish, my arse."

"Um! You're not allowed to say 'arse.'"

"Arse, arse, arse," muttered the older girl. "Fish are for eating."

The girl named Aimee appeared unperturbed by the outburst. "My Dad says I swim like a fish now."

"My Uncle Zane says I play rugby like a pro."

"That's cool, Etta."

Etta grinned. "Yep! Sure is." With obvious affection, she ruffled the younger girl's blonde curls. "And so are you. Come on, cuz, let's go and get some kai. I'm starving."

They both turned and saw Maddy at the same time. "Hey," said Aimee. "Who are you?"

Before Maddy could answer, Etta spoke.

"You're Maddy, I remember you from before. Your Gabe's *friend*." Etta put a cheeky emphasis on the word "friend" which Maddy decided it was best to ignore.

"Yes, that's right."

"Hi, Maddy!" said Aimee. "Do you want to come with us, and I'll show you where Aunty Rachel is? She's in the kitchen. She's always in the kitchen," she said, extending her hand trustingly.

It was on the tip of Maddy's tongue to say she'd been working here over the past few weeks, long enough to know her way around, but she didn't want to turn down Aimee's kind offer. Besides, this was Jonny's niece. A niece he'd last seen as a baby.

The two girls were as different as chalk and cheese, Maddy thought as she accepted Aimee's hand and all three walked up to the house. Aimee chatted all the way. It was only a few minutes' walk but by the end of it Maddy knew that her mother was Lizzi, the eldest daughter of the Connelly clan and that her new father was Pete and that they lived in the Mackenzie country and that Aimee was going to be a champion swimmer and that her Uncle Max and Auntie Laura were going to arrive in a helicopter.

It was the one thing which made Etta listen. "A helicopter? That's pretty cool, eh?"

"Yes," said Maddy. "I guess it is."

Etta stopped. "I'm going back to the beach. Are you coming, Aimee?"

Aimee was torn between politeness and the novelty of bringing a grown-up to the house and having some fun.

"Why don't you go with Etta?" helped Maddy. "I'll find my way from here."

"Okay," said Aimee. "All you need to do is follow the smell of the food, anyway." She laughed and ran down the steps to join Etta.

Maddy caught a whiff of sensational food wafting from the house, and her mouth watered. She walked up the steps of the veranda and looked around. No one else was in sight, but she could hear someone moving around inside. She called out, but there was no response, so she stepped through the open door and walked into the large kitchen.

A woman stood at the chopping board, her dark hair piled gloriously on her head, and her curvaceous figure shown off by the figure-hugging knee-length dress. She looked like an Italian film star. At that moment she looked up with dark eyes—eyes that Maddy had been bracing herself to see since she'd arrived in Akaroa, and seen Jonny's sister on the television. And now she saw what she'd been both been dreading and eagerly anticipating—Jonny's eyes, on his sister Rachel.

Rachel smiled, and Maddy had no choice but to do the same.

"You must be the elusive Madeleine. We barely exchanged a few words last time you were here, but Gabe's told me all about you. Are you hungry? He said you have a good appetite."

Maddy laughed. "Please, call me Maddy. And I bet he said I'm always hungry."

Rachel raised an eyebrow. "Maybe."

"That doesn't sound very complimentary."

"It does to me. I like hungry people. Without them, I'd be out of a job! Come. Help yourself to a glass of wine—there's some in the fridge—and tell me all about yourself."

Maddy readily did what Rachel suggested. Rachel was like Jonny in that way too. She had a natural authority. It was interesting seeing who took after whom. It gave Jonny a context—a place within the world which she'd been ignorant of before.

Maddy finished pouring out two glasses just as Rachel put the dish into the oven and set the timer. She rose and wiped her hands on the cloth. "There, now we can talk before everyone descends."

They didn't go outside but sat in the window seat of the kitchen overlooking the lawn which ran down to the beach where the two girls were now swimming. Rachel sighed, her eyes focused on Etta. "I can't tell you how long I've waited for moments like these." She laughed as Aimee splashed Etta, and Etta restrained her natural boisterousness to splash Aimee back.

"Like this?" Maddy asked, puzzled. It seemed a very quiet kind of moment.

Rachel turned away from the window and looked at Maddy. "It probably doesn't seem much to you. Very domestic—food in the oven, a husband arriving shortly, and my child playing on the beach with my niece. But it's all I've ever wanted, and it took me a long time to find it."

Rachel's openness touched Maddy. "It's good to know what you want."

"It's even better to get it!" Rachel's eyes narrowed as she sipped her wine. "But don't you know what you want? I'm sure you do, deep down."

Maddy shrugged, suddenly feeling uncomfortable. "I guess I enjoy my job, I like to travel."

Rachel cocked her head to catch Maddy's eye. "But? I sense a 'but.'"

Maddy drew in a deep breath to give herself courage and looked Rachel in the eye. "But, no, I don't know what I want. Or rather, I think I do, but I'm not sure I should have it."

"Should have it? Who's to dictate what you should, or shouldn't have?"

Maddy grimaced. "Someone from my past."

"Ah." Rachel leaned back against the sofa. "Is that person likely to show up in the present?"

Maddy shook her head. "No. He died."

"I'm so sorry."

Maddy swallowed and shrugged, unable to say anything.

"And so you feel guilty that you might want to move on?"

Maddy nodded. In the distance she heard some cars enter the drive, followed by the bang of car doors, and voices calling out in greeting.

Rachel ignored them, and reached out and took Maddy's hand. "It's difficult for you. But time will make it easier. And talking about it."

"Thank you. Yes, I realize that, but knowing it doesn't seem to make me feel any better."

"No, but you will." Rachel rose and glanced out the window and waved to someone who Maddy couldn't see. "They're here." She looked back at Maddy. "Promise me one thing. Go easy on Gabe. He likes you."

"And I like him."

"No, but he *really* likes you, in a way I haven't seen Gabe like anyone before. So, as a fond sister, I'd ask that you don't hurt him. If you don't think you can commit, you might want to let him know, before he gets in any deeper."

"Of course." That was the second family warning she'd received, suggesting she shouldn't hurt Gabe. Jim and Rachel didn't realize that she didn't need warning, because she didn't want to hurt him.

She followed Rachel outside where all the family had arrived, including Gabe, intensely aware that everything was about to change. Time was running out.

GABE IMMEDIATELY NOTICED Maddy standing behind Rachel and knew that they'd had a serious chat. He wished his family wouldn't keep meddling in his business. He'd never minded before, but it was different this time.

While the introductions were being made, Aimee, Etta, and the dogs emerged, dripping from the sea, and the dogs shook their wet coats over everyone. Maddy looked more ill-at-ease than ever amongst all the chaos. He longed to reach out to her, to squeeze her hand, to ask her if she was okay, to draw her to one side and find out what the matter was, what fears and doubts were passing through that beautiful head of hers, but he could do none of these things. She wasn't his date and didn't want to be. She'd made that very clear.

But he was her friend. He stepped forward, ignoring his family, and spoke directly to Maddy. "Have you been shown around the house, Maddy?"

She shook her head. "Not really. I've spent most of my time in the grounds."

"Would you like me to show you around Belendroit?"

Her face flooded with relief as the noisy family settled down and words flew between them. He opened a door, and Maddy gratefully slipped into the darkened room. He closed it behind him. She looked around with a strangely keen curiosity. The room was dark after the bright light outside and he watched the tension ease from Maddy's shoulders.

"This is the library. A bit dusty, but Dad won't let anyone do anything about it. We call it his 'shrine.'"

"Will he mind us being here?"

"Not at all. Dad might not want anyone throwing anything out, or tidying up, but otherwise what's his is everyone's. It's family stuff." He walked over to the arrangement of photos. They weren't beautifully arranged and dusted, but clumped together. Finger marks were visible where they'd been recently picked up. Gabe grunted. "I see Dad's been looking at the last photo of us all together before Jonny left." He grimaced and held it out for Maddy to see. "I don't think he'll ever get over his death."

Maddy took the photo from him, and her eyes moved over the individual members of the family. "You all look quite different. There's a similarity between some of you. Who are these two at the back?"

Gabe looked to see where she was pointing and grinned. "Rob and Cameron. They never seem to understand that you should smile in a photo."

Maddy smiled, but it didn't reach her eyes. "I think you were smiling for all the guys."

"Yeah, Jonny didn't have to do a thing. All eyes were on him anyway." He glanced at Maddy. "Like yours."

She looked up suddenly and he was shocked at the intensity he saw in her eyes. She looked away again as quickly and handed him the photo.

Slowly he replaced it on the shelf. He felt strangely disappointed that Maddy should be like all the rest, focused intently on his twin brother. "Would you like to see the rest of the place? It's pretty old and has been rebuilt using even earlier timbers. I think the archaeologist in you might be interested." He kept talking, as he tried to make sense of the expression he'd seen in her eyes. It was like she'd seen a ghost. He wanted it gone. "And the estate, too. But then you know all about that, don't you? Dad said you and the university team had already made a start on the dig."

He walked over to the door to the hall and opened it wide. Evening sunlight flooded in, breaking the spell. She looked up, and the light robbed him of the ability to read her eyes. It reflected back to him as she glanced at him and passed through into the hallway.

They sat down on the veranda with the others. Gabe was relieved to be back with his brother and sisters. Something was wrong—out of place—but he didn't know what. Maybe by watching Maddy interact with his family he could find out what.

"So," asked Lizzi, with a welcoming smile. "What did you say do for a living, Maddy?"

Maddy sat where indicated and accepted a glass of soda water from Gabe. "I'm an archaeologist." She'd always found it easier to tell people the bare minimum about her work. Any more than "archaeologist" and people's eyes glazed over. But Gabe had different ideas.

"Maddy specializes in Geographic Information Systems."

Lizzi narrowed her eyes. "Geographic Information Systems? What's that? Sorry, I'm so unscientific, it's not funny."

"Maddy, you'll have to take it from here. I've gone to the limits of my knowledge."

She shook her head. "Really, it's not very interesting."

"Then why do you do it?" asked Lizzi.

"Well, I mean it's interesting to me. But..." Maddy sighed, realizing she hadn't managed to avoid the science speech. "Okay, basically it takes unrelated information and relates it by using location as the key index variable."

Somehow she'd managed to arrest every conversation and all eyes turned to her. She smiled uncertainly.

Lizzi's nodded encouragingly, despite the fact she clearly had no understanding of what Maddy had just said. "Go on," she said politely.

Maddy hated the fact that everyone was looking at her. She shrugged. "It relates earth-based spatial-temporal locations to—" She paused to see the reaction. It wasn't good. Lizzi's smile had become fixed; Pete sighed and looked down. "I mean, it helps archaeologists," she added.

"Oh," said Lizzi and Pete together, relieved that they understood a word. "You know, Maddy, you should meet one of my best friends. I have a feeling you and Rebecca would get along well. Don't you Pete?"

Pete grinned. "Sure. She's a science nerd, too."

"Pete!" said Lizzi, flicking him on the arm. "You'll have to excuse my husband. He's only interested in science as far as his wine crop goes, and nothing more. Like me and my cooking, I guess. I know as much as I need to make sure ingredients work well together, and that's my limit."

Jim barked out a sharp laugh. "You see, Maddy, I told you my family wouldn't appreciate your skills."

"And I suppose you do, Dad?" asked Lizzi.

"Of course. I've always subscribed to National Geographic."

"Oh well, then, you're an expert," Lizzi continued.

"Now, don't be facetious."

"Well, really, what do you know about archaeology?"

"A darn sight more than you do." Jim turned to Maddy. "Shall we show them?"

She grinned. "I reckon."

Gabe turned from one to the other. "What have you two been up to?"

"Not only us two, eh, Madeleine?"

Maddy and Jim led the way off the veranda, down the steps, across the short stretch of lawn toward the woods. At the far end, hidden from the house by the trees, they stopped in front of the trench.

"Wow! You didn't hang around!" said Gabe, amazed, as he paced from one end of the trench to the other.

"Careful!" said Maddy. "Don't stand too near the edge. You need to keep behind the markers!"

"Okay," said Gabe stepping away, but peering inside. "So what's been going on, then?"

"We've discovered the remnants of post holes of what we think is a blockhouse, as well as examining the remains of middens. There's a lot of stuff here."

"Dad! It's brilliant that you've let them dig here, after so long. What changed your mind?"

Jim looked at Maddy with a gentle smile. "I couldn't resist Madeleine's explanation of why we should dig here."

"What was it?" asked Gabe.

"Madeleine?" Jim raised an eyebrow. "Perhaps you'd care to repeat your persuasive argument?"

"Just that uncovering the past is important," said Maddy. "We can't move forward until we know what went before. It's important—especially so here, where these people were most likely your ancestors." She looked around from one stunned face to another. "They're your family. You can't just forget they existed. We need to know them. We need to know what happened to them."

Maddy had been speaking from the heart and hadn't been thinking specifically of Jonny. But when she looked around at the faces of the Connelly family, she realized something had happened. The atmosphere had changed. Lizzi turned away abruptly, and Pete put his arm around her. Rachel looked anxiously at Gabe. And Gabe? He was looking at her with a look of complete and utter disbelief on his face.

"What did you say?" he asked.

Maddy repeated what she'd said and, after a glance at his father, Gabe shook his head.

"Anyway," said Jim rubbing his hands together. "Time for dinner." He walked away with the others, leaving Gabe and Maddy alone.

Maddy looked at Gabe. "What did I say?"

"Something which reminded us of Jonny, that's all. An open wound still."

Gabe changed the subject and they walked back to the house. But his words repeated in her head. She couldn't put it off any longer; she'd have to tell him, and soon.

9

It was late now. Maddy paused on her way back from the kitchen as Lizzi's voice drifted down the hallway. She was trying to settle an over-tired Aimee whom she and Pete had awoken as they'd retired to bed. Maddy listened to Lizzi sing a song to soothe Aimee back to sleep. It was a Simon and Garfunkel song which Maddy remembered her uncle playing—*Are you going to Scarborough Fair*. An odd choice for a lullaby maybe, but Lizzi's sweet voice must have worked because soon there was no sound coming from the bedroom which all three were sharing.

And Lizzi's song had an odd effect on Maddy, too. She also felt strangely soothed. Or maybe it was the light of the moon which was high now and bathed Belendroit in silver. Amongst the trees, lanterns hung, lighting the driveway up to the road. Or maybe it was the quiet, indistinct talk coming from the veranda. Light in the dark, the comforting sounds of family around; whatever it was, it sent a delicious shiver down Maddy's spine. She looked through the open door, hesitating on the threshold, not wanting that feeling to leave, not yet. Seated in the glow of half-a-dozen candles were Jim

Connelly, Max and Laura, who lay along the cushioned seat, her head in Max's lap, as he played with her hair.

They were talking about Laura's new challenge, and Gabe was teasing her and Max about their inability to lead a quiet life, only to receive a heap of teasing back from Max.

"You guys! Quit teasing!" said Laura, sounding almost shocked by the banter.

"Don't worry about them, Laura," said Jim. "If they didn't drive each other to distraction I'd think something was wrong. Gabe honed his skills early, with Jonny. They used to drive their mother crazy with their arguing and fighting." He turned to Max. "Do you remember all that business over Gabe's toy car, Max?"

"I wish I could forget it," said Max. "It was like the third world war."

"Toy car?" said Gabe. "It was not just a toy car! It was a Batmobile. I loved it. I'd saved up my earnings—"

"You had earnings as a kid?" Laura laughed. "What did you do?"

"He used to help out at the vet's surgery, didn't you, Gabe?" replied Max. "If my little brother wasn't sticking plasters on Amber while she lay in her crib, he was rescuing animals and taking them to the local vets."

Gabe grinned. "I think they got so fed up with me bringing them injured animals, they thought they'd better occupy me inside the vets. Cleaning out the cages, mopping up the excrement and vomit."

"Ew," said Laura, screwing up her lovely face. "That sounds gross."

"Yes," admitted Gabe. "It does. But I loved it." He glanced up and saw Maddy perched on the arm of a chair inside the study, watching them, and smiled, apparently understanding her need to be apart for a while. He turned back to Max. "I guess I've always had a gross side."

"What you have, dear brother, is a caring side. In fact, I don't think it could be described as a 'side.' It's just you. Through and through. Like a piece of rock candy, you have 'caring' imprinted on your core."

Gabe grunted. Maddy knew by now that he didn't like to be praised, or be the center of attention. "I didn't feel so caring when Jonny nicked my Batmobile."

Maddy suddenly had a sinking feeling in the pit of her stomach.

"Why did he do that?" asked Laura.

Gabe shrugged. "He wanted it. But don't worry, I nicked it back again."

"And so it went on," Jim said to Laura. "The twins' bickering used to drive Mary to distraction. I used to tell her to ignore it; they were boys being boys. But she was scared they didn't love each other."

"We loved each other," Gabe said quietly. Maddy had never seen such an expression on his face before. He usually covered his feelings and emotions up with a cheery persona, but now she could see the similarity with Jonny, now she could see the depths of his feelings for his twin brother. "We just weren't very good at showing it."

Jim grunted. "I'm going to see what's left in the fridge. Anyone want any cheese?"

After collecting orders, Jim disappeared inside.

Laura sat up and stretched out her hand and touched Gabe. "I'm so sorry for your loss."

Gabe looked up, startled. "Everyone's loss."

"But especially yours. They say a twin's bond has depths that no one can understand."

The glow of the evening had faded for Maddy, leaving only a sense of responsibility. She'd tell Gabe later tonight. It was time. No doubt after she'd told him he'd think it was past time.

Needing to get away, Maddy walked around to the rear of the house which overlooked the water. Rachel and Zane were sitting on the back deck looking up at the stars, while Etta enjoyed a midnight swim.

Etta suddenly waved and shouted for Zane, who jumped up with athletic ease and jogged down to the jetty. Rachel followed him and Maddy sat on the bench they'd just vacated, looking out across the moonlit sea. Her mind drifted back to the time Jonny had first told her about Belendroit.

It had been in a café in Amsterdam, and she'd run in to meet him, kissed him and proceeded to talk about a friend she'd just bumped into, at the same time sipping from the beer he'd ordered. She had taken her a good five minutes to realize that something was wrong. He'd been too quiet. He'd never been too quiet—the result of growing up with seven noisy siblings and two noisy parents, he'd always claimed. But she suspected it was simply who he was—noisy, vivid, alive. She'd asked him what was wrong, but instead of telling her he'd described Belendroit.

He'd taken a sip of his usual glass of red wine and described the view from the back deck of his family home. How in full sun the glare of the light on the water had you pulling down the rattan blinds his mother had hung, diffusing the light, making the veranda into another room. But then, how at midnight, the new moon would rise directly opposite, peeping over the hills and casting a silver light across the water. Apparently, it was a family tradition to swim into it, creating little stars of bioluminescence in their wakes. He'd explained that the effect—neon-colored stars and exploding flashes—was stronger when there was no moon, but the eerie glow was still there in late summer when the water was warm enough.

And that was what was happening now. Zane had stripped off to his shorts, and joined Etta in the water, swimming strongly out toward the pontoon which was moored just off the point. Rachel stood on the jetty, watching them.

She hadn't understood at first why Jonny had told her this in such vivid detail. But then he told her, with increasing agitation that he was convinced he was going to die young, despite all her arguments to the contrary. He'd been obsessed with the idea of family and insisted on her agreeing to visit Belendroit and make amends to his family for the things he'd done in the past. He'd only calmed down after she'd agreed to do as he asked—visit Belendroit for six months, at the end of which she should tell them about her and him. She didn't think for one minute it would ever eventuate, especially after he went back on his medication. But within a month he'd gone, leaving her with nothing except a promise to keep.

There was a shout, and Rachel laughed and returned to her chair beside Maddy. Maddy was brought back to the present with heart-wrenching suddenness. She blinked and surreptitiously swiped her fingers under her eyes.

Rachel turned with a smile which froze on her lips. "Are you okay? Anything the matter?"

Maddy cleared her throat and shook her head, hoping that the light was sufficiently dim to cover her sadness. "No, I'm fine. It's just so beautiful, isn't it?" She looked firmly out to sea, hoping Rachel's gaze would follow suit. It did after a few seconds, lured by the sight of her husband and daughter swimming in the calm sea, illuminated by bright blue flashes of light.

"It sure is." Rachel said. "I can't believe I waited so long to return home."

Maddy suddenly felt anxious. She opened her mouth to speak—anything to change the subject from home and family—but thoughts formed briefly before evaporating into the night, and Rachel beat her to it.

"I wish Jonny had told us where he was, what he was

doing. Anything. And I wish he hadn't argued with Gabe that night; I wish that I knew something of his life after he'd left us." Rachel looked up at Maddy with tears in her eyes. "So many wishes. But all I know is that he left in a fury, and died without any message, without any attempt to reunite with us." She retrieved a handkerchief from her pocket. "I'm sorry, but we've all tried not to say anything, or do anything, to make it worse, but somehow it's worse not saying anything."

Tentatively, Maddy reached out and squeezed Rachel's hand. It was all she could do for her before her own heart broke. "I'm sorry."

Rachel blew her nose and smiled a smile that was too bright. "Nothing for you to be sorry about! But thank you, anyway."

"It's okay. It's okay," she repeated, unable to bear it any longer. She jumped up and pulled her cardigan closer around her. "I have to go. Thanks so much for everything."

Rachel tried to laugh through her tears. "Everything? It was just dinner! Dinner followed by a few tears. That doesn't deserve your thanks."

"You know it was more than that. And I have to leave."

Rachel frowned, and also rose. "That sounds very final. It's not, is it? You're not going anywhere, are you?"

Maddy hadn't meant to be so obvious, but it was too late to backtrack. And she couldn't do that to any of the Connelly family, especially not Rachel. She shrugged as she tried to frame unframeable words.

There was a sudden shout from Etta. "Mum!"

Rachel looked over with a smile before turning back to Maddy and taking her hand. "Tell me, is everything all right between you and Gabe?"

"Sure," Maddy said. "Sure," she said, more strongly this time. "You go."

There was another call, and she could see Rachel was torn. "Are you sure?"

"Sure, I'm sure."

"I'll see you soon, then." Rachel jumped down the steps and went running onto the jetty to where Etta was pushing herself out of the water, shivering slightly. Maddy stood watching as, after Rachel helped Etta out of the sea, Zane put up his hand and pulled Rachel into the water with a splash. After an initial squawk, things went very quiet as Etta ran back up the jetty toward the house, oblivious to the meaning of the lack of sound coming from the water.

That was love, Maddy thought to herself. Pure, uncomplicated love. How she wished it could be like that for her.

Maddy walked up the beach toward the house and hesitated before joining the others. She was more aware than ever that she was an outsider here, and didn't feel able to join them. Instead, she listened to Etta responding to questions from Laura of whom she was totally in awe. Etta was talking about the rugby scholarship she hoped she'd receive in the US one day. The conversation broadened into all of their hopes for the future. The family was all so certain, so confident, that Maddy knew without a doubt their hopes would eventuate. She didn't think she could ever recall possessing such confidence. And yet it existed in abundance in Belendroit. Even the adults had retained that confidence. Or, with some, maybe they'd mislaid it along the way, but re-found it again.

"You look lost." Gabe's voice drifted to her, and she looked up to see him, half-hidden by the wisteria at the end of the deck, looking out toward the sea.

"In thought, maybe," she said climbing up the steps to him. "But not lost."

He reached out for her hand and pulled her to him. He pushed back her hair from her face. "That's better, now I can see you." He pretended to inspect her face. She could almost feel the trail of his gaze, as if it were a feather teasing sensation from her. He smiled as he noticed her reaction and tilted her chin to catch the candlelight. "I think you're wrong. I think you *have* been lost, but now you've been found."

She opened her mouth to deny it but before she could speak his lips pressed to hers. Her remonstrance turned into a gasp as his tongue slid against hers. She melted against him, and his arms grew stronger to support her. The kiss grew in intensity as their bodies pressed hard against each other. Hot desire ignited deep inside her, fanned by the pressure of his hand pulling her against him. She wanted his hand to move lower, she wanted the kiss never to end, she wanted him, completely.

It was the sound of people emerging on the deck around the corner to them which eventually made them pull apart.

Gabe cupped her face and kissed her again briefly on the lips. "Will you stay with me tonight, Maddy?"

Yes, she'd stay with him, and she'd tell him everything. She couldn't postpone it any longer. It wasn't fair to Gabe, and it wasn't fair to her, either. She'd done as much as she could to keep Jonny's promise, but enough was enough.

She nodded. "Yes, I will."

"Let's go and say our goodbyes."

As Maddy said goodnight to the Connellys, she couldn't help thinking that this could be the last time she saw them. After tonight Gabe would know about her and Jonny—as would the rest of the Connellys, no doubt—and just like the Connellys usually did, they'd rally around their brother to protect him, and shut her out. And she deserved it, of course. She'd kept a secret from them, one which she doubted they'd ever forgive her for.

She waved her last farewells to the family, and to Rachel

and Zane who were finally emerging from the water, and walked quickly toward the beach path.

"Are you okay?" Gabe asked, sensing her strange mood.

"Sure," she smiled. "I had a lovely evening. But..."

"But you found my family a bit too much at times? I saw you taking time out in the study. Listening to us, but for some reason wanting to stay in the background."

She shrugged. "I'm an introvert, through and through. I need my alone time."

He grinned and put his arm around her. "And you can have it... so long as I'm allowed to be alone with you."

Maddy pressed her head against his shoulder. "Sure can. So long as you're quiet."

His chuckle vibrated through her cheek, and he kissed her hair. "I can't promise total silence."

She lifted her head, and he turned her in his arms. "That's good, nor me."

He kissed her, and her world kaleidoscoped into that one thing—his lips on hers, moving, cajoling, caressing. She would have agreed to anything at that moment but he suddenly pulled away, and the real world fell back into place around her.

He brushed his thumb across her lips. "We'll never get home at this rate." He took her hand, and they continued walking. "Talk to me."

"About what?"

"Anything to get my mind off the idea of ravishing you on the beach."

"Oh! Is that such a bad idea?"

"Maddy," Gabe growled. "You're not helping."

"Well, I don't know what to talk about!"

"Ask me a question."

"Okay..."

"Anything you want to know about me."

"Right. There is something." She glanced at him to see his reaction. "Why aren't you married?"

"I nearly was. To Juliet."

"Who's Juliet?"

"Before your time."

Jonny hadn't told Maddy anything about Gabe's love life except that he was hopeless at it. That he only fell for mysterious women who he needed to protect, but they'd always been seriously flaky. "So what went wrong?"

"I realized I wasn't the right man for her."

"In what way?"

"In the only way that mattered."

She waited for him to elaborate.

He stopped walking and turned to her. "I didn't love her. Not enough, anyway. And I could never marry someone whom I didn't love. It wouldn't be fair, on either of us."

The night insects chirruped in the native bush behind the trees which lined the path. It pulsed with a sense of expectation.

"Was she upset?"

"Yes. She thought we should marry, and that I'd grow to love her."

"Ah, that's sad."

"Yes, and it was hard to tell her that I thought that wouldn't happen."

"You did the right thing. I don't believe time has much influence on feelings."

"What do you mean?"

She shrugged. "Just that you can know within a short span of time whether you love someone."

He grunted in surprise. "Yes, you're right. So there's not much point in waiting is there? Not when you know for sure."

She frowned, not understanding.

"Will you marry me, Maddy?"

Of all the things she'd imagined he was about to say, this hadn't entered her radar. "Marry you? Gabe!"

"I know it's sudden, but what's the point in waiting when everything is so right. I love you. You must know that by now. And I think you might love me too."

She shook her head. This wasn't meant to have gone like this! She needed to tell him something, explain things to him, not listen to a proposal of marriage from him.

"Are you at a *complete* loss for words?"

She shook her head. "No, I have words, but I think they're the wrong ones."

His face fell. "I don't understand."

She rubbed the heel of her hand against her forehead, willing it to ease the tension which had sprung up. "Maybe, for the moment, I don't want you to."

"You don't want to marry me."

"No, I don't. But that doesn't mean that I don't have feelings for you."

"Feelings? That's pretty vague. My patients have feelings for me; and I'm sure our spaniels have feelings for me."

There was only one way to show him how deep her feelings went. She lifted her face to his and kissed him, trying to put everything she felt, but couldn't allow herself to say, into that kiss.

He pulled away before she was ready and pressed his forehead against hers. "Okay, so your feelings are different to our dogs."

She grinned. "We need to talk, Gabe."

"Then talk."

She looked around. A dark path in the middle of nowhere wasn't the place for what she had to say. "Not here."

"My place? A glass of wine and a chat?"

She nodded and stepped away from him, releasing his hands. "Sounds good."

They walked the rest of the way without touching, their conversation resolutely sticking to neutral ground, as if neither dared trust themselves with anything personal.

But it all changed when they arrived at Gabe's house. The minute they walked into the narrow hallway, Maddy brushed against him as he held the door open, and he raised his hand and caressed her arm. Startled, she turned to find there was no longer any gap between them. She couldn't have said who kissed whom, but the effect was dramatic. Within seconds a passion was ignited from which there was no going back.

Their hands were over each other's body, tugging at the clothing, searching for the hot skin beneath, their breathing coming faster as they stumbled toward the bedroom. Their mouths were too busy for further words, and they fell onto the bed as one.

THE FIRST THING Gabe did when he awoke was to feel for Maddy. But his hand clenched around the sheets, not the sensuous, responsive body he'd spent the night exploring. Somewhere, deep inside, he'd known she'd be missing when he awoke.

When she'd rejected his proposal, he'd reasoned to himself that he'd surprised her and that she'd come round, because he could have sworn that she felt for him the same as he felt for her. But now he had to admit that, as amazing as their night together had been, she'd been holding back, and that she obviously didn't intend to accept his proposal of marriage.

"Maddy?" he called, trying to keep the desperation out of his voice. "Where are you?"

There was no reply. He jumped up and walked into the

hall, checking the bathroom, before walking, naked into the kitchen. He looked outside. The house was small, so it didn't take long to confirm she wasn't in it. He pushed his hands through his hair and went into the bathroom. He needed to find her; he needed to tell her that she *had* to stay, that six months wasn't long enough, that no time would be long enough. He splashed water onto his face and gripped the sink and didn't recognize the gaze that looked back at him. Gone was the nonchalant, happy-go-lucky persona which was a part of his personality, but not all of him by any means. But it had been easy, it had been convenient, and it had made him and those around him happy. But all that had disappeared when he realized he was madly and deeply in love with Maddy.

Suddenly he heard the front door open and the sound of jandals flip-flopping against the wooden boards in his hall. The door was kicked closed with a foot as if she were holding something. It banged shut. He waited for the panic to subside from his eyes before he left the bathroom and stepped out into the hall.

"Hey, you!" greeted Maddy, eyeing up his naked body. "I thought you'd like something to eat." She grinned. "Just as well you're not expecting any patients before nine, otherwise they'd have got more than they bargained for!" Maddy frowned at the lack of a response from Gabe. "Is everything all right?"

He shrugged and walked toward the bedroom. "I'll go get dressed."

Maddy followed him into the bedroom as he pulled on his jeans. "What's the matter, Gabe? Has anything happened?"

"*You* happened, Maddy. *You*." He plucked a clean shirt from the wardrobe.

"And I seem to have made you sad."

He held her gaze as he buttoned up his shirt. "I thought you'd gone."

"I wouldn't go without saying goodbye."

He grunted and looked at her. "So is that coffee simply for adornment or can I have one?"

She gave a weak smile and passed him a cup. "Amber added an extra shot. She said she thought you might need it."

He shook his head and opened the door for her. "That woman. I think she knows what's going on around here before everyone else, including those involved."

"Yeah," said Maddy, exiting the door ahead of Gabe. "If I believed in things like that I'd say she had extra-sensory perception. But as I'm a scientist, I reckon she's simply observant."

Gabe opened the back door and sat on the step and sipped his coffee. He knew Maddy was talking more than usual because she was nervous. But he wasn't in the mood for making things easier for her. He knew what was coming, as surely as Amber would have done.

She put down her bag and picked up her coffee and hesitated. "Would you like company?"

"Of course." He moved along the stone step which was already warm from the morning sun.

She sat down, and he took a deep breath. She smelt of coffee, cinnamon and something altogether richer and more womanly which made his mouth water, but now wasn't the moment to indulge himself. He had a feeling it would backfire. Instead, he sipped his coffee and waited. Waited for the inevitable.

"Gabe." Her voice was soft and gentle, imploring even. He hated being implored.

He turned to her. "Yes, Maddy."

"About last night."

"What about it?"

"I'm not so sure it was sensible of me to have stayed."

"I'm not sure sense came into it."

"No, I guess you're right." She took another sip of coffee. "But I'm glad I did."

"Glad? I'm bowled over by faint praise."

"You know I'm hopeless at saying important things. And this is important. Last night was amazing." She looked away with a frown as if trying to figure out how to express something unpleasant, or complicated. He hoped it was the latter. "Making love to you was more than physical. I felt a connection with you which I never—"

She stopped herself abruptly. He reached out and took her hand. "You don't have to say anything."

She looked at him for the first time since she'd begun speaking and he was taken aback to see tears in her eyes. "I do, Gabe. I do because..." She trailed off. He thought it about time to lighten the atmosphere.

"Because you want to go back into the bedroom and give me a chance to be on top for a change?"

Suddenly from over the wall came the sound of a throaty cough. "Morning, Gabe!"

Maddy swore under her breath and ran inside, leaving a trail of coffee after her. Gabe liked having close neighbors—he *really* did—but there were times when he wished he lived in the middle of nowhere, like at Belendroit.

"Morning, Fred. How are you this morning?"

"Not as good as you, I reckon!" laughed Fred.

Gabe groaned. "Pretend you didn't hear any of that, for my sake, will you? Or else that's all my patients will be talking about."

"Sure thing, Dr. Gabe, whatever you say." Fred went laughing back inside his house, and Gabe knew that the news Dr. Gabe had a thing going on with his accounts clerk would be broadcast far and wide as soon as Fred entered the pub. Gabe had three hours.

With a sigh, Gabe went back inside. Maddy was standing at the kitchen sink, pouring the remains of her coffee down the sink. He closed the door firmly behind him.

"Sorry about that. One of the downsides of having close neighbors."

But she wasn't smiling when she turned around. "You don't mind about that, do you? You don't mind about living your life in full view."

He shrugged. "No. I've nothing to hide, so why should I mind?"

She smiled then. "I had a similar conversation once with someone who replied with the same comment."

"Wise man."

"Yes, he was."

There was something in the way she said that which made Gabe's stomach sink. He opened his mouth to speak, but his mouth was too dry. He licked his lips. He had a feeling that she was about to tell him why she couldn't stay. He cleared his throat. "Who was he?" But even so, the words came out hoarse.

"He was Jonny, Gabe. Jonny, your brother, your twin."

He opened his mouth, but no sound emerged. He felt weak and sat down on the arm of a chair and just stared at her. "You knew my brother Jonny?"

"Yes."

"You knew, and you didn't tell me? You've only just decided to tell me now? What the hell?"

"I couldn't tell you."

"Couldn't, or wouldn't?"

"Couldn't. He didn't want me to. Not until the six months were up, anyway."

"Six months? So this was all some weird plan concocted by you both?"

"No. It was the weird plan *he* concocted. I just agreed to it. He *made* me agree. He began talking about it when he'd reached rock bottom mentally after coming off his medication. He was convinced he was going to die. He was obsessed with the idea, and he wouldn't let up about it until I promised him I'd come here.

"What?"

"Come to Akaroa, to meet you, and the rest of his family, and to stay for at least six months."

"Why the hell did he want you to do that? Hey?" He gripped her arms now, wanting to force the truth from her. "Why?"

"He wanted me to give you something. Please, let go of me, and I'll get it."

He hadn't even realized the force with which he was holding her. He looked down at his hands and dropped them to his side. "I'm sorry." He turned and pushed his hands through his hair. He gripped the kitchen bench and closed his eyes, his mind full of Jonny's face. His twin, his best friend, the brother who'd left New Zealand full of rage, never to return. He felt his brother's betrayal all over again, with double force this time. Because it included Maddy.

"Here."

He turned around, hardly remembering what it was she was doing. She was holding something out to him. He shook his head. "What is it?"

She hesitated. "I know what it is. What I don't know is what it means." She continued to hold it out, but he didn't take it. Just looked at the wrapped lump in her hands without interest. "But I'm guessing it means something because Jonny didn't do things on a whim."

"Except leaving here. No, wait. That wasn't on a whim.

He'd always said he was leaving, and he had no idea why I wanted to stay." He looked at her. "But then I'm guessing you'd know that. How long did you know him?"

She dropped her hand and placed the object on the table between them. "I knew him for two years."

"Two years!" He hadn't expected that. He shook his head in his hands. What the hell was happening? It was like a Pandora's box had opened up, and he had no clue what would happen next. "How could you be with me for the past few months, with me, with Amber, with us all, and not tell us that?"

"He didn't want me to tell you. He expressly asked me *not* to tell you until I was about to leave."

He flinched as if he'd been struck. It was the final stab in his heart. "Why don't you go now?" He rose and turned his back to her. "Just go now."

"Don't you want to know more about Jonny? About our life together?"

"Why? So I can think of the two of you together after you've gone? Think of you making love to him as you have done to me." He laughed hollowly. "Christ, what a fool I've been. It was some last trick of his, wasn't it? He always wanted the last laugh, and he's got it now. And he's not even alive to see it. He sent you to deal it to me. Go. Go now."

She reached out and took hold of his arm.

"I'm sorry, Gabe. I'm so sorry."

He frowned. "For what?"

She didn't speak.

He gripped her hands in hers. "For what, Maddy? For what? For being in Akaroa, for flirting with me, for me falling in love with you?"

She shook her head and tried to pull away from him but he wouldn't let her go.

"What's the matter? Surprised to see that the easygoing Gabe Connelly has feelings?"

"No, of course not. I know they're there. And I know that you hide them from so many people, but not me anymore."

"Maybe I should have done," he said quietly. He closed his eyes and swore under his breath. "Go now."

He walked outside and waited until he heard the front door close and the flip-flop of her jandals hit the hot dry pavement in the street outside.

"Didn't expect to see you back outside so quick!" said his neighbor who popped up with a bright grin on his face.

"Yeah, well some things don't always go to plan," said Gabe. "See you later, Fred."

He returned inside and poured himself a large whiskey. He rarely drank spirits, and never so early in the day. He'd seen too many of his friends become slowly addicted to it. But he needed a shot of something to dull the pain that coursed through his body and throbbed in every cell, every fiber of his being. He was in pain, and he felt stupid, humiliated by a brother with whom he'd always competed, tricked by a woman with whom he'd fallen in love. He'd been had all right.

10

It wasn't until much later, after hours of ignoring knocks at the door, of texts, of phone calls, that his friends and family left him alone, presumably thinking he'd gone away. Luckily there was no medical emergency, and the other medical practice was open. So Gabe was eventually left alone to watch the day fade.

The sun lowered in the sky, sending its searching beams across the room. Gabe poured himself another whiskey. He'd spent all day looking at the object which still sat on the table where Maddy had left it.

Maddy, or Jonny's fiancée, as she should have been known.

It was a further hour before he picked it up. After he'd unwrapped it, he'd placed it back on the table again. He'd known what it was before he'd unwrapped it. He just hadn't wanted to admit it.

The antique eighteenth-century astrolabe had been found buried on the shore near Belendroit. The astrolabe—the ancient forerunner to a compass—must have been a treasure owned by one of the captains, rather than relied on for navigating the southern ocean, because it had been superseded by the time European boats had found their way here. For centuries before the exploration of this land, it had been used to help sailors find their way—to faraway adventures, and then home again. The significance of Jonny returning it to Gabe wasn't lost on him.

Years ago, they'd argued over which of the twins had discovered it. Jonny had claimed it was him who had found it washed up. But it hadn't been that way, and Jonny knew it. It had been Gabe, who'd been digging for Pipis, who'd found it. It had been *his* treasure, and he'd cherished it. Their mother had insisted they share it. From their early teens Gabe and Jonny had fought all the time, being so close and yet so different. But when Jonny had packed to leave, Gabe had given him the astrolabe. Jonny had accused him of giving it to him to weigh down his luggage, but he'd known, he'd understood. Gabe had given it to Jonny because he loved him, and he wanted to share the thing he cherished most, the thing that they'd squabbled over most.

A knock at the door followed by the rattle of a door key broke Gabe's reverie. He groaned. The only person who had a key was his father. Gabe didn't move but heard the familiar stomp of his father's footsteps down the hall.

"Gabe!" came the peremptory bark. "Gabe? Where the hell are you?"

Gabe took another swig of whiskey and pushed his hands through his hair, irritated to have his seclusion broken. "In here."

He heard his father's equally irritated grunt as he stopped by the door, hands on hips, and looked at his son. "Drinking," he said with derision. "As if that's a cure for anything." He stepped into the room, picked up the whiskey bottle and squinted at the label. "Hm, quite a good label though." Without asking, he took the bottle to the cupboard and plucked out a glass and poured himself a healthy measure.

"I hope you're not driving," said Gabe.

"I'll catch a lift with Amber later." He sipped the whiskey and narrowed his eyes as he swirled it around the glass. "Hm, not bad." He set it down on the table, made himself comfortable in the chair, and looked directly at Gabe. "Well then?"

"Well then what?" Gabe wasn't in the mood for surrendering his innermost thoughts to his father. He'd have to work for them.

"Why are you holed up here on your own with only a bottle of whiskey for company?"

"I like whiskey."

"No you don't. Not this much anyway. It's Maddy, isn't it?"

Gabe shrugged. "Now why would you think that?"

"Because Maddy told me about her and Jonny."

Gabe stared at his father as if he was seeing him for the first time. Jim flicked an imaginary speck of fluff from his trousers and casually swirled the whiskey and took another sip.

Jim gave Gabe a double take. "Don't look at me like I'm an alien. I do know what's going on around me, you know."

"Really?"

Jim grunted. "Well, maybe not all the time, but this time I do."

"So tell me what it is you think you know."

"I know that Madeleine was with Jonny when he died, that they were," he paused, "together."

"Together," repeated Gabe with derision. "'Together' doesn't begin to describe their relationship."

"If you're the expert, you tell me then."

"Maddy was living with Jonny."

Jim didn't say anything.

"Maddy was Jonny's lover."

Still, Jim didn't speak.

"Dad! Don't you understand what I'm saying?"

Jim pressed his lips together and reached out for Gabe as he stormed past, his mind and heart ablaze with fury and confusion. But Gabe continued walking, ignoring his father's hand which tried to stay the movement and the fury.

"I understand what you're saying, son."

"Then how come you're not reacting?"

His father again didn't say a word. But his eyes spoke for him. Gabe suddenly understood.

"You knew before Maddy told you." He shook his head and looked around, unable to believe it. "You damn well knew and didn't say a word."

"I promised Madeleine I wouldn't."

"You'd rather promise someone you hardly know than reveal such an important secret to your son?"

"It wasn't my secret to tell."

"No," Gabe said, unable to prevent a bitterness creeping into his tone. "It was Maddy's. And Jonny's. But you knew, too, somehow. Tell me, how was that?"

"I remembered her surname. It was in your brother's will. I only remembered it because it's the same as a friend of your mother's. No relation of course, but still, it stuck in my head. And that, together with the fact that she'd been living in Amsterdam, and had turned up here. Just one too many coincidences."

"Yes."

Gabe sat down, his head in his hands, all fight gone, only despair remaining. "I can't believe it. The only time I fall in love, it's with Jonny's ex." He grunted. "Some way for Jonny to bridge the gap of his parting, sending his fiancée as a token of his love for me."

"Is that what you think that was? A token of his love for you?" Jim shook his head. "No, boy, don't you see? He obviously adored Maddy and wanted her looked after. And who better to look after his most cherished treasure, than the other person he loved most in the world?" Gabe began to remonstrate, but Jim put up his hand. "Let me finish. You boys were twins, and as a doctor you know full well what that means. You began life together which made the split which followed harder to bear than most. You were close, son, closer than anyone I know."

Tears pricked Gabe's eyes. "Then why did he leave, and not come back?"

"He made a mistake." Jim shook his head and picked up the astrolabe. "A mistake; an error in judgment, compounded by his illness. That's my guess anyway." He held it out for Gabe to take. "But he's back now. He's given you the most precious things he has, and he wants you to cherish them, and in so doing, cherish your and his connection, your love. Don't let pride stand in your way like it did when he left. That was one thing you both shared—pride. Don't do it." He rose. "*That* is my advice to you. The rest is up to you."

Jim knocked back the rest of the whiskey and gave an appreciative sound before nodding to Gabe and leaving the room, his steps heavy on the polished floorboards. The door banged shut, and Gabe was alone once more. But something had changed. It was like finding that final key to unlock the whole truth, and re-arranging the pieces, so they suddenly formed a coherent picture. His father was right. It wasn't all about him and Jonny; it was about Maddy.

He understood now.

Maddy couldn't settle. She'd sorted out the accounts at the Backpackers and left a detailed list of instructions for Flo to follow once she'd left. Then she'd gone for a walk, fingering her cellphone ten times a minute, tempted to ring, tempted to text, but doing none of those things. She'd done what she'd told Jonny she'd do. The rest was up to Gabe.

She peeled off her clothes and ran into the sea to cool her heated head and heart, needing to wear out the agitation which filled her. But as she walked along the wind-whipped beach, the warm air drying her, it had no effect.

She glanced up the beach to Belendroit, its lanterns sending a ripple of light across the water. Guiding lights to ensure the family's safe return home, Gabe had said. Not for her. She'd be leaving tomorrow, and it was up to Gabe whether he wanted to hear any more of her and Jonny's story.

She returned to the hostel and told Flo that she was hanging out on the beach that evening, refusing the company which Flo offered. Instead, she took a beer and nursed it on the beach. It wasn't until the moon had risen over the hills that she heard a noise behind her. Some sand rose in the air and stung her eyes. She jumped up and turned around.

"Gabe!"

"Maddy," he said. "Flo told me you'd be here."

"I texted you and told you, too."

"Ah, well. Unlike my brother Jonny, I'm not wed to my phone." He barked out a dry laugh. "Ha! Funny. He wasn't only wedded to his phone, was he?"

"We weren't married," she said quietly.

"No. He died before you *could* marry."

She heard the hurt in every syllable. She flexed her hands into fists to stop herself from reaching out to him. "I didn't think you'd come."

"No, well I didn't think I'd come either. But I guess I didn't want a repeat of when Jonny left. The barest of communication until we were notified of his death."

"He was going to get in contact. I'm sure of it. I think to begin with he'd wanted to cut loose and then he'd gotten sick. But he was recovering and had been talking about you all."

"Talk." He grunted dismissively. "He was always good at talking. Except not to his family." Gabe sat down beside her and looked out at the dim horizon. "Do you know what it's like to be a member of a large, tight-knit family and have one of you disappear like that? It devastated everyone, especially my sisters."

Especially Gabe, she thought. "It devastated him, too. Except he didn't admit it to himself until he got sick."

Silence descended, and she looked at Gabe as he gazed out into the mid-distance, his mind thousands of miles away. His hair lifted with the brisk breeze, and the smell of a nearby barbecue drifted down the beach to them. She shivered. Then he looked at her for the first time. She hadn't thought he'd notice her shiver, but he had.

"You're cold." He pulled off his jacket and put it around her shoulders, his fingers lingering as he smoothed it over her. Their gaze caught and tangled before he looked once more toward the sea.

She opened her mouth to speak but thought better of it.

"What were you about to say?" he asked.

She bit her lip but held his gaze. "That Jonny used to do that."

Gabe nodded and looked away again. "Of course he did. He loved you, and he sent you here, to me, because he wanted me to love you, too."

"How could he? No, that wasn't it. That would have been crazy."

"Not if you know the other person as well as a twin does."

She shook her head vehemently. "No, he simply wanted me to heal the rift between you. He wanted me to be the conduit, a bridge between you both, to help you to heal."

"Don't you see, Maddy? It was more than that. He wanted me to fall in love, and I obliged. Trouble is, I'm not Jonny."

"What do you mean?"

He stirred himself to look up at her as if his mind was far away. "You loved *Jonny,* not me. He imagined you could switch allegiances, fall for me too, and ta-da, neat happy ending. But real life isn't like that."

She couldn't begin to tell him what real life was like so kept silent.

He laid the astrolabe out on the sand before them. "I loved this thing as a kid. I found it and kept it safe for a long time, refused to let anyone play with it in case they damaged it. And when Jonny got hold of it one time he knocked a chip off it." He held it up to the light. "See, here?" He traced a thin line of white with his finger. "Here's where I tried to glue it back together. I was eight years old and had a bench space on Dad's garden shed where I mended things. I loved it."

"So how come Jonny had it?"

He looked up and shook his head with a smile. "He always loved beautiful things." He paused as his eyes swept her face and hair. "So I gave it to him as a kind of peace offering—a way of remembering what we had. We loved each other, we fought each other's battles, and what was his was mine, and mine his. We were always there for each other." He bit his lip. "Except at the end. When he needed me most, I wasn't there."

"How could you have been? He didn't tell you where he was." She shook her head. "And the end was the result of a stupid accident which no one could have foreseen." She huffed. "Except apparently Jonny. You couldn't have been there."

Gabe's gaze focused back on her. "But *you* were there." His voice was quiet. It wasn't a question, but rather a resigned statement that showed his sadness that she had a past she hadn't revealed to him, and a past that was intimately connected to his family. She felt ashamed of her duplicity all over again.

"Yes, I was there."

He indicated the bench. "Let's sit down under the tree, and you can tell me everything."

The breeze off the sea had quickened and tossed the branches of the pohutukawa tree, creating crazy criss-cross moon shadows on the silvered wooden bench, upon which lovers' names had been carved beside knots in the grain which had been weathered by rain and sand and wind. They sat across from each other and Maddy felt the distance keenly. She fingered one of the knots as she tried to collect her thoughts.

Gabe leaned his arms on the table and didn't take his eyes off her. "Go on, Maddy."

"I'm trying to work out where to begin."

"Let's start with where you met Jonny. After he left New Zealand in such a dramatic rush, we didn't hear from him for ages."

"That must have been hard."

"Yes. We knew he was backpacking around Europe but little else. For a while he sent us regular postcards, which had jokes, light-hearted comments on them, but nothing really about the life he was living. Then he told us he'd got married and was expecting a child. My sisters were devastated he hadn't invited us to the wedding."

"Jonny told me it was an impulse registry office wedding. And that they were separated shortly after his son was born."

Gabe pressed his lips together and looked down. "That

was Jonny—all impulse and no sense of responsibility. Tell me how you met him."

"It was in Amsterdam. I'd finished a contract at the university there and had arranged to hang out with some friends for a few more weeks before moving on."

She faltered as she relived the memory of her first meeting with Jonny.

"Go on."

"I noticed him as soon as he walked into the room with a small group of friends. He lit up the room. And, then he looked at me, and that was it." She shrugged, unable to describe the intensity of what had happened next.

Maddy glanced at Gabe who briefly closed his eyes before picking up a stone and throwing it into the sea. He sighed. "You fell for each other."

She didn't raise her lashes but continued to tease out a knot of wood on the bench top. "Yes. It would have been hard not to fall for Jonny." She bit her lip, wondering if she should continue. But one glance at Gabe's haunted eyes, and she decided not to. He rubbed his forehead with the heel of his hand as if trying to rid his mind of images of herself and Jonny.

"So... did you stay in The Netherlands?"

"For a while. But he wanted to explore the world, so we left after a few months."

"Where did you go?"

"We headed East. Jonny had tired of the Amsterdam scene. He'd been mixing with the wrong crowd, taking drugs. At first I thought some of his more extreme behavior was because of them. It was only later..."

"Ah, so it wasn't until later that you got to learn of his problems."

"Yes. He hid it well. But I knew something was wrong

when he kept on wanting to travel away from the West. He had some sort of phobia about it."

"And, I'm guessing, it didn't stop."

"No. It got worse."

"Was he still taking drugs?"

"I'm not sure. If he was, I didn't see him take them. But later I found out that he should have been taking medication."

He reached out and touched her hand. "Jonny was diagnosed bi-polar shortly before he left the country. It was what drove him away. We tried to make sure he took his medication, but I'm guessing between the drugs he took in Amsterdam and lack of prescription medication in the East, he stopped."

She looked up and saw a reflection of her own pain in his eyes.

"Were you with him at the end?"

"Yes. He died in hospital; I was at his side."

"That must have been hard."

The raw pain that was behind the tears nearly ripped her cool apart. "Yes," she mouthed, unable to speak. She cleared her throat and swallowed. She had to keep it together; she had to tell him everything. "I couldn't believe it. He'd been improving; he'd been talking about home, but had some morbid premonition of death."

"His bi-polar talking."

"Probably." Although she still couldn't help believe it was something more. "And because of that, he made me promise to come here."

He picked up the astrolabe and turned it in his hand. "To come to Akaroa, track me down, and return an ancient, dysfunctional, out-of-date piece of memorabilia to me."

"Yes. I thought it sounded crazy then, and it sounds even crazier now." She pulled her hands away and swung her legs off the bench. "I'm sorry, Gabe. I should never have come. I've wasted your time, and I've only made you sad."

He rose and stood beside her and looked out to sea while she pulled a tissue from her pocket and swept the tears from her cheeks and blew her nose.

"You haven't, you know," he said at last.

"What?"

"Wasted my time. You knew Jonny what, for a couple of years?"

"Yes."

"And I knew him for twenty-two years, until his diagnosis and his disappearance. I was born first and apparently stopped screaming when he emerged. He started screaming as soon as he was born, and I stopped. And that's how we went on. We were inseparable for years. We shared the same bedroom, the same hobbies, the same humor. I knew him, Maddy, I knew him, and I hunted for him after he left, tried to find him, but couldn't. And you telling me what you know about him, how he lived the last two years of his life has meant a lot to me. It's completed a story which I kept trying, but failing, to complete. It's brought some closure, I guess. Closure on something that had closed over a year ago. So, no, you haven't wasted my time."

"Good. I'm glad. I guess Jonny knew that and that was why he wanted me to come here and find you."

"No. Now *there* you're wrong. Sure he wanted me to know. But it's more than that. Don't you know why he wanted you to come here?" He tossed the astrolabe in his hand again.

She shook her head, suddenly off-kilter. She'd come to Akaroa to tell Gabe about Jonny. It was her with the secret, not Gabe.

"I think the recurrence of his bi-polar symptoms scared him," said Gabe. "He loved you."

"What makes you so sure? Sometimes it didn't feel like that."

"No, he loved you. I know that for sure because we always loved the same things."

She looked up sharply at his acknowledgment that he still loved her, and she knew from the intensity in his eyes that, despite everything, he *did* still love her. He reached out and pushed a strand of hair behind her ear. His face flickered with a wince or a smile—Maddy couldn't have said which—as he touched her cheek before pulling away with a sigh.

"He *loved* you," Gabe repeated. "And he wanted you cared for if anything happened to him. And I've always cared for things, for people; that's what I do."

She shook her head as she tried to comprehend what Gabe was saying, and jumped to her feet. "No. No, that's not it. He wanted me to come here purely for you, for your family, for me to heal the rift, to tell you that he loved you."

"Listen to me, Maddy." Gabe took hold of both her hands. "Jonny wanted me to fall in love with you, and I have. He wanted me to cherish you, as *he* couldn't cherish you, and I do."

All the strength drained from Maddy's body, and she crumpled to her knees on the wet sand and heard the sound of loud, uncontrolled sobbing. It was shocking to her, not least because it was coming from her and she hadn't a hope in hell of controlling it. She tried to fight off Gabe's arms but gave up instead and pressed her cheek to his chest while he held her and let her sob.

"It's okay," he said as he tenderly pressed his lips to her head. "It's okay."

But it didn't feel okay. She'd thought she'd been sent here for Gabe's sake, not her own. But now the memories, the words of the past flew through her mind, stopping only to confirm Gabe's statement. She should have known. She should have realized, but she hadn't. It had taken Gabe's knowledge of Jonny—their shared bond which hadn't been severed, despite the distance between them—to make her see.

Slowly the sobbing subsided, and she pulled away from him.

"It's okay," Gabe repeated, releasing her from his arms.

She nodded and dug into her jeans for another tissue and blew her nose. She nodded again and cleared her throat. "I guess it will be okay." She sent him a watery smile. "Just doesn't feel like it yet."

"And I will, Maddy, if you let me."

She frowned, trying to follow his train of thought.

"I will," he repeated, "cherish you, if you'll let me."

She loved him; she knew that now. But did she want her life to be arranged for her by Jonny? Jonny had taken control of her life from the moment they'd met. From giving up her work, to where they lived, the decisions had been his. Did she really want Jonny's influence to extend beyond the grave and to predict her future?

Gabe stood up and held out his hand to her. She accepted it, and he helped her up. "But I don't want to know if you'll let me yet. Only when you're ready. Now, come on, let's go back to the Backpackers and see if Flo can rustle up some tea for us."

GABE KEPT his arm around Maddy as they walked back to the Backpackers. He was worried about her. He'd never seen her like this, so exposed and raw. He knew that an infected wound could be hidden by newly formed skin, and overlooked. And that sometimes that surface had to be taken away and the raw wound revealed for it to heal. And Maddy had to heal, she had to grieve for Jonny. And all he could do was give her time.

Back with Flo, they drank tea in a shocked, aching silence. Maddy didn't want Flo to leave, and so Flo tried to fill the silence with talk about inconsequential things—from how well her veggies were doing in the garden, to the local amateur dramatic production in which Jim Connelly was starring. Gabe watched as Maddy nodded vaguely when Flo talked about the difference that having the archaeologists staying had made to her cash flow, and to the future of her business. Maddy sighed as Flo continue to talk about how she'd already put out feelers to banks and potential backers to fund some of the more ambitious plans. Then, eventually, even Flo fell silent and turned to them.

"I don't know what's going on with you guys, but you need to sort it out."

Maddy bit her lip and glanced awkwardly at Gabe. "I don't think we can, Flo. It's too difficult."

"We could try, Maddy," said Gabe, refusing to leave without a fight.

"You could," said Flo enthusiastically. "Don't do what I did, and be too proud to put things to rights when things went wrong."

"What things?" asked Gabe, wondering if she was talking about his brother, Rob.

"None of your business," said Flo, closing the subject. "The details aren't important. What is important is that I let my stupid pride stop me from accepting an apology. I had this ridiculous sense of how things should be, and if they didn't match up, then there was no point." She reached over and deadheaded a rose. "God, I was stupid." She allowed the fading petals to fall one by one from her hands onto the wooden veranda. When she looked up, there were tears in her eyes. "And I've regretted it every day since."

Maddy put her arm around Flo and pulled her to her side in a swift hug, but Flo had recovered rapidly and pulled away —independent to the last. She rose. "So," she said more brusquely, pointing her finger from one to the other. "I don't want to see you two stuffing up something beautiful, like I did. Right?"

They both muttered something, as Flo walked off, apparently satisfied. Gabe rose and moved opposite Maddy, deliberately sitting back, not offering sympathy, not offering anything that could sway her decision. The cards were on the table, and it was up to her to do what she wanted with her hand.

She looked up with eyes which were far away, still with Jonny, and his heart sank. "So, where to from here?" she asked.

But he wasn't giving up without a fight, even if it wasn't the fight she might have been expecting. He wanted those eyes on him. Always.

"Forward. That's where," he said briskly, standing up with sudden decision.

"I don't know if I can. I feel like I've taken you for a ride, that I've tricked you and your whole family in this crazy charade I agreed to with Jonny. I'm so sorry, Gabe. I feel so ashamed. I should never have agreed."

"It's okay."

"Really?"

"Yes. But only if you agree to my terms."

"Your terms?"

"Yes, you agreed to stay in Akaroa for six months for Jonny. You lasted three months before telling me. Now I want you to do the same for me. I want you to stay for three months in Akaroa. Continue the life you've created for yourself here for a further three months."

"But what's the point? Why on earth would you want me to do that?"

"Haven't I made myself clear? I love you. I want you in my life. As loathe as I am to admit that I've reacted just as Jonny had predicted, the truth is that I have. I want you to stay to complete the six months. If you think you owe me, then you can make it up by staying another three months. What do you say?"

She rose, too, and stood in front of him. It was all he could do not to reach out and pull her into his arms and keep her there. How could he make her see that she should be with him, not the memory of his twin brother?

"What do you say?" he repeated. He could hear the force in his words which was unusual for him. Forced and husky with urgency and need.

She nodded. "If that's what you want, it's the least I can do."

He'd have preferred something more enthusiastic, but he'd take what he could get.

"Okay."

She drew in a deep breath as if for courage and exhaled. "So, what do you want me to do?"

"I want you to carry on just as you have been, making connections with people, healing. Just as Jonny wanted."

"And at the end of the six months? What then?"

He backed away, only pausing at the steps down to the road. He glanced around. "We'll see." And then he walked away, his mind full of Maddy's face, clouded with confusion. She'd thought she'd been sent here for him, and Gabe was sure that there was an element of reconciliation involved in the promise Jonny had forced on Maddy. But he instinctively knew it was more than that, and his father had confirmed his instincts. Jonny wanted him to look after Maddy, to cherish her as he no longer could. And, despite the shock around her revelation, Gabe knew he would, as much as she would let him.

But would she let him? He knew what he felt for Maddy, but the question was, how much did she feel for him? He had three months to find out.

11

A bead of sweat trickled down Maddy's back as she paced the open grassy area between the woods and Belendroit, focusing intently on the piece of machinery she was holding. When she reached the edge of the woods she stopped, checked the readings and flicked the switch. Done.

Maddy leaned against a tree trunk and looked around. The late afternoon sunlight flooded the trees overhead, their golden leaves scarcely moving in the still heat. She looked across the site to the last of the team who were preparing to leave. They were her kind of people—dressed in drill shorts, stained shirts and hats and gumboots—practical, good-humored and passionate about their work. She hadn't realized how much she'd missed the work, nor the people.

They waved and mimed a drink at her, and she waved back.

"I'll see you there."

There was no reason for anyone to ask where "there" was. There was only one place where all the archaeologists went to after work—Flo's Place, as it had become known. Many of them—particularly those from overseas and temporarily homeless—had found a home at Flo's Place for the duration of the dig. And, in the process, had turned around the profit for Flo. At least Maddy had been of help there, she thought.

Maddy pulled off her cap, wiped the sweat from her forehead and pushed her fingers through her damp hair. It was hot—hot and humid. Everybody felt the oppression of the approaching storm. Even the most patient of the team had thrown down his trowel in exasperation as a promising lump had turned out to be just that—a nondescript lump. She looked across the harbor to a leaden sky which reflected its intense blue-gray onto the sea's surface. Time to pack up for the day before the storm hit.

She stowed the equipment and sat on the step of the shed for a while looking over the dig, feeling a sense of peace she hadn't felt for a long while. She'd come a long way since she'd arrived in New Zealand. The past few months—with the archaeology, and friendship, and getting to know Jonny's family—had given her a sense of perspective and, despite all that she felt for Jonny, she could now see how Jonny had manipulated her. From the moment that they'd met when he'd dominated her by force of personality alone, to later, when she'd wanted to return to work, and he'd persuaded her otherwise, he'd been in control. Between the sheer intensity of his personality and his effective ways of persuasion, she hadn't stood a chance. But now she could see more clearly, and she refused to allow herself to be manipulated anymore. It wasn't fair to her, and it certainly wouldn't be fair to anyone else. What was the old expression? If you loved someone, you should set them free. It wasn't what Jonny had done. But it was what she would do for Gabe. She felt she'd been forced on him, as much as he'd been forced on her. And neither scenario was healthy. He wanted her to stay, but she couldn't. So all she had to do was to find the courage to tell him that. She brushed the soil from her fingers and gave a brief, empty laugh, knowing, deep down, that Gabe wouldn't understand. But she had to try to make him understand. She owed him that much.

She rose and brushed off her shorts and waved goodbye to the last departing member of the archaeology team. She'd be seeing them all later at the hostel. And Gabe. It was one of the team's birthday, and Flo was laying on a party for them. She'd tell him then.

"HOT ENOUGH FOR YOU?" called Edie, an elderly patient of Gabe's from across the road.

"Sure is!" replied Gabe. "This summer is going on and on."

Edie looked across the hills to where the sky was dark. "Looks like rain. I wouldn't be surprised if we have a thunderstorm later."

They exchanged a few more pleasantries before Edie continued on her way. Gabe glanced at the sky as he walked on toward Flo's house. Edie was right. The atmosphere was odd. There was a sense of expectation, an electricity in the air. He just hoped it wouldn't affect Flo's party because he had plans.

A couple of weeks had passed since Maddy had told Gabe about herself and Jonny. Maddy had continued to stay at Akaroa although she'd never actually agreed to Gabe's request. He was just relieved she'd stayed, and had taken it as a sign that he still had a chance. And he was determined not to blow it.

He fingered the jewelry box which contained the ring he'd selected from an exclusive Christchurch store. He'd had it a week now and had been waiting until the right moment, which meant a moment when Maddy wasn't engrossed in her archaeology work at Belendroit, or surrounded by other people. There would be lots of people at tonight's party, but he was hoping that afterward, they would be alone. He had a bottle of champagne chilling in the fridge, just in case.

He paused at the gate to the Backpackers when he saw Maddy seated with the others on the veranda. She hadn't noticed him appear in the prematurely dark evening, as he stood outside the fall of the street light. He took a deep breath to calm his nerves. It was ridiculous. He'd never been this nervous around a woman before. But, then he'd never proposed marriage before. As he watched her it struck him that, while the others were conversing, Maddy wasn't joining in. He doubted she even heard what they were saying. She appeared cool and aloof, just as she had when he'd first seen her. He looked away, hating to see her like that—as if there was a barrier between her and the rest of the world, as if she were afraid of it. What could she be afraid of now?

The gate clicked as he opened it and she turned to him and smiled, and he fingered the ring box again. Perhaps he was wrong. Perhaps everything would be all right.

"Gabe!" called Flo. "Come and join us and grab a beer on the way. They're in the ice bucket out on the deck."

Gabe plucked a beer from the now slushy container and went to join them. Flo wriggled over and made a space between her and Maddy which Gabe immediately took. He smiled and was relieved to see the separateness that was so characteristic of her disappear. "How are things?" He was gratified to see a heat come into her eyes and a flush to her cheeks which had been missing before.

"Good, thanks."

"And the dig?"

She pulled a face. "The dig is fine. We're getting some great finds. But the university wants me to front a TV programme to publicize it." She shook her head. "I hate that kind of thing."

He didn't doubt it. She wasn't like his sister Rachel, who

was totally at ease in front of a camera. "You would be perfect, Maddy. You wouldn't have to pretend to be anybody you're not. They want someone passionate about the work, and you are that. Why not give it a go?"

She grimaced. "I don't like the idea. I'd rather be getting my hands dirty than speaking to a camera."

He took a swig from his beer bottle. "Then why don't you refuse?"

She shrugged. "I don't want to let anyone down."

He swilled his drink around the bottle, suddenly uncomfortable again. Was this how it was always going to be with Maddy? Her agreeing to things she didn't want to do because she felt she owed people for some reason or other? Would she feel the same way when he proposed to her?

"You should do exactly what you want. Why don't you find out what's involved, and if you still don't want to do, tell them? No doubt you could contribute in other ways. Don't do what you don't want to do, Maddy. It's not fair on anyone."

She turned abruptly to face him, and he could see that she understood his broader meaning. She licked her lips as if struggling with how to respond. Then she looked at him firmly. "But I'm here right now because you asked me to stay around."

His heart sank. "Is that the only reason you stayed? Tell me the truth. Don't tell me what you think I want to hear."

Maddy shrugged, her bright hair falling over her face, obscuring her expression, as she watched someone emerge from the house with a guitar, and begin to play a plaintive Irish melody. Cicadas throbbed in the trees and the sky darkened further as clouds rolled in from the north, trapping the day's heat and intensifying it. But still she didn't answer, and the silence was filled with Flo's voice, as she joined the guitarist in a song whose emotions could be felt without needing to understand the Gaelic words she sang.

By the time the song had finished Maddy still hadn't broken her silence, and he found his bottle was empty. She placed her hand on his and wrapped her fingers around his and squeezed them. She leaned into him so that only he could hear what she was saying.

"Partly. I *do* feel I owe you." She shook her head when he was about to remonstrate, and continued. "But... it's complicated." She shrugged.

"I need to know, Maddy. I *need* to know." He swallowed, feeling the weight of the velvet box in his pocket. "It can't be *that* complicated."

"It is. But I have a shortened version."

"Don't keep me guessing," he said quietly.

She gripped his hand again. "I stayed because of you. Because I want to be with you."

With you, he repeated the words in his mind. *With you*. It didn't exactly smack of undying love. He tried to forget the ring box in his pocket.

She rose. "Do you fancy a walk?"

He was surprised, but there was no way on this earth that he'd refuse. "Sure." He tried to sound casual, more like Jonny would have sounded.

They made their excuses to Flo and slipped away.

Under the starless sky and air that barely moved, the sea sounded restless as the waves broke on the shore, providing a welcome coolness.

Maddy slipped her hand into his. Since the night, two weeks before, when she'd told him about her relationship with Jonny, they'd continued to be physically close, holding hands, the odd kiss, and he knew that she had feelings for him, but he hadn't pressed anything, and she hadn't revealed anything. But now, for some reason, he felt a tension in the way she held herself, and the way she held his hand.

"Which way shall we go?" he asked. He knew where he wanted to take her—straight to his place—but wanted it to come from her.

She cocked her head to one side and smiled. "Your place?"

He nodded, understanding. Something had changed, and whatever it was, if it meant spending the night at his place, then he was fine with it. He was suddenly aware once more of the ring box.

The five-minute walk seemed to take longer than it usually did. Sheet lightning lit up the horizon, and a distant rumble followed, but the rain held off. Gabe was preternaturally aware of every glance, every move of every muscle which Maddy made. He felt with a sinking heart that maybe his instincts knew better than he did. That she was going to leave and that he was trying to capture her in his mind, where he could remember her when she'd gone. It was going to be goodbye—but it appeared she was in no hurry to say that goodbye. It was exquisite—both the pleasure and torture of her company. He never wanted it to end.

He closed his front door and was about to flick on the light when Maddy placed her hand on his. Another flash of lightning filled the hallway; her face was so close to his that he could see his dark shadow reflected in her eyes. He stepped away, not liking how his darkness filled her. It wasn't what he wanted. But Maddy moved toward him, bridging the gap he'd created. He shook his head and stepped away again. And again, she countered his movement with one of her own. He hadn't the control to take her hand from his arm, where her fingers dug into his muscles.

"Maddy! I don't know why you're here, or what you want from me. Just tell me straight."

"Straight?" She gave a small huff of a laugh. "I don't think

I can, because I'm not sure I know anymore. All I know is what I feel here, now. And I want to be close to you. Gabe, I want to make love with you."

It might not have been the declaration of love he'd hoped for, and he knew the ring box would stay in his pocket. But, he thought as their mouths met in a kiss that was as feverish as the weather outside, if this was going to be their last night together, he'd make damn sure it was one she'd never forget.

As Maddy listened to the hall clock strike three in the morning, she shifted carefully on the bed, so as not to wake Gabe, acutely aware of the delicious tingle in every square inch of her body. Gabe had made sure of that. But while the passion they'd shared had sated her physical needs, it had done nothing to unravel the confusion that filled her mind. She hated that she couldn't tell Gabe what he wanted to hear. But she couldn't continue the charade which Jonny had created.

She sighed, wondering how on earth she could do what she had to do, without hurting the people she loved most in the world.

"What is it?" asked Gabe softly.

She turned to find him looking at her, the outline of his face barely visible in the dim light. Just a denser black against the gray-black of pre-dawn. How long he'd been lying awake, looking at her, she didn't know. He hadn't moved. His arm was still under her head, his hand still on her hip. She stroked her foot up his calf and shifted on her side to look at him.

She opened her mouth to say, "nothing", but closed it again without speaking. "Nothing" didn't come anywhere close to describing what troubled her. "Everything" would have been a more accurate answer.

"If I had to guess I'd say you were wondering how you could extricate yourself from me, from here, from us all." She opened her mouth to reply, but he pressed his finger gently against her lips. "Hear me out, Maddy. I want you to stay."

"I'm not going anywhere at three a.m. It's cold out there," she added with a brief smile. But her light tone didn't make him change his expression.

"Stay," he repeated.

His hand reached out to hers, and he kissed it, before holding it up to the dim light, turning it as if examining it, as if it were something rare. She turned her head on the pillow to look at him, but his eyes were only on their joined hands.

She opened her mouth to speak, but the words wouldn't form, and she closed her mouth and her eyes. She felt the touch of his fingertip on her lips, and she opened her eyes. "It's not that simple."

"It can be if you want it to be." His roving finger finished with a swift caress of her cheek.

He was wrong; nothing was simple, not in her heart or mind. And it wasn't fair on Gabe. "You deserve better than me."

He grunted. "Do I? And I wonder what you think you deserve?"

She shrugged, unable to begin to unravel her thoughts and feelings, scared that he'd misunderstand. So she resorted to her usual shorthand—aloof indifference. It had served her well so far. She rolled her head back on the pillow, her gaze fixed on the ceiling with its dense shadows. She tried in vain to quiet her heart. "An easy life."

"Don't do that, Maddy. Not to me."

Her smile faded. She should have known he'd see through her facile comment.

"You think you're so perceptive."

"That's because I am. You may be right; you may not be good enough for me, but I still want you."

"No, Gabe. It's no good. It doesn't feel right."

"Because of Jonny."

"Partly, but also because of me."

"My brother could be a pain in the arse, but he was a clever man, and a loyal and loving one. He wanted you cared for, looked after, cherished, by someone he trusted. Whatever went on between us, he always trusted me."

She tilted her head back on the pillow and remembered the night Jonny had asked her to come here. She swallowed hard. "I thought I was a messenger of last resort. Someone to heal the rift, someone to show you that the person closest to you in the world loved you, despite what had happened."

"Maybe that, too. But whatever, you're here with me now, thanks to Jonny. We can only guess at his motives, but I think it's pretty clear he'd approve of us being together."

She ground her teeth, trying to rein in her emotions.

"Stay," he repeated. "Stay with me forever."

She shifted to look at him and knew what he was asking. The small jewelry box she'd seen in his pocket; the champagne in the fridge and that look in his eyes. And she equally knew what her answer had to be.

"I can't, Gabe. Don't you see? I can't stay. I need to leave. I feel like I've been placed on a roller coaster by Jonny which has changed my life, my direction, even me. But it's time I took control of my own life. I can't stay. Not while there is confusion and doubt in my mind."

He swallowed and lay back, his eyes on the ceiling. "Of course."

She flinched at the dead, cool tone of his voice. She'd hurt him, and she couldn't let him know that that hurt pained her more than anything. "I have to tell you one more thing."

He sighed. "What's that?"

"My love for Jonny was... complicated." She said the words so softly she hardly heard them. But, when she turned to look at him, she could see he'd heard them from the puzzled look on his face.

"Complicated? How?" He twisted around until he was facing her. She didn't move, but continued to look up at the ornate plaster rose on the ceiling, from which the central light hung. She traced with her eye the thickly painted contours until she'd been around them all.

She sucked in a difficult breath, frowning as she remembered. "At first, I was dazzled by him and surrendered myself totally for him." She narrowed her eyes. "Now I look back on it, I'm not sure it was a healthy kind of love. It was unbalanced somehow. And the longer I was with him, the more my doubts grew." She shook her head. "He knew. I think he must have known. But there was no way I could leave him... not like that." She broke off abruptly, no longer able to trust her voice as the tears pooled in her eyes and slid down her cheeks, soaking the pillow.

Gabe's arm slid under the pillow and he swept her into his arms where she unleashed her sobs into his chest while he continued to hold her until there were no more tears. All that was left were empty hiccupping sobs which he absorbed into his body, trying to relieve her of the pain of loving one brother more than the other.

GABE AWOKE the next morning to the sound of a window clunking against its frame, and rain drumming at the window— the first hint of autumn. It wasn't the best of omens. And nor was the empty bed beside him.

"Maddy?" he called as he got up, pulled on his jeans and went in search of her.

But even before he'd finished checking each room, he

knew the house was empty. He felt her absence as if it were a physical thing. He drew the curtains and looked out at the sea which pulsed up and down the shore in an agitated rhythm, reflecting the stormy gray skies and scudding clouds.

He clicked shut the window, whose banging had awoken him. But he could still hear the roar of the sea, and the keening of the wind as it struck the overhead wires. The heat from his palm condensed on the glass, obscuring the trees which bent over, and revealing his reflection—dark shadows under haunted eyes. He grunted. Hardly surprising. Haunted by a twin brother who refused to have anything to do with him in the last years of his life, and now he was dead, refused to leave him alone.

"You're a bastard, Jonny."

The window blew open again. He swore, and fixed it yet again, looking up and down the empty, windswept, rain-lashed street, for signs of Maddy. Then he saw her—a flash of white-blond hair bobbing on the far pavement, heading toward the sea.

He quickly pulled on his oilskin jacket and stepped out into the street, buffeted by the wind as he walked to where he'd last seen her. The sea had taken on a different, sinister character this morning. There was none of last night's lulling passivity, only a barely repressed fury, as the high seas sent sprays across the pier and road. He saw Maddy walking along the pier and followed her. She walked quickly toward a shelter and disappeared from view.

He briefly wondered if he should leave her to do whatever it was she wanted, but now wasn't the time to avoid anything, it was the time to face everything.

He found her sitting looking out to sea, sheltered from the blustery northerly by a wall of windows. She looked cold and numb. He sat down on the damp seat beside her and followed her gaze across the turbulent gray water to the hills across the harbor, their tops shrouded in mist.

"So you may not have loved him as he loved you," he said. "That's not a crime."

"Then why does it feel like one?"

"Because you're a kind person, and you didn't want to upset him, or his memory."

"Kind!" she spat out. "How can you believe me to be a kind person when I seem to leave a trail of disaster after me?" She looked at him with eyes full of pain, and it nearly broke his heart.

"Because you are. It wasn't your fault that Jonny fell madly in love with you. And it wasn't your fault that he fell ill. And it wasn't his either. It was just"—he threw his arms out—"life. Fate. Stuff that happens. And you have to move on from there."

She looked around like a caged animal, and then back at him with fierce eyes, an expression he hadn't seen in her before. "After my uncle died I kept moving on. And that didn't work out for me so well. I made sure I made no friends, no connections, nothing and no one who would touch me, in case they left me again. And then I met Jonny."

"And you stayed with him, and he left you, too. But not before sending you to me."

She nodded. "I stayed and perhaps I shouldn't have."

His heart sank. He opened his mouth to speak but the words dissolved and fled before he had the chance to utter them. There was only one thing he needed to know.

"Tell me, Maddy, how do you feel now?" His voice was quiet and urgent, as he willed her to understand what he was asking. But one look at her and he could see that she was still caught up in a whirl of emotions, only some of which related to him.

"How do I feel? I feel that everyone needs something from

me; seems everyone is trying to put me in some place or other. Jonny insisted I keep a promise to come here. I thought it was for him. But it seems he wanted to manipulate me after his death, too—"

"*I* don't want to manipulate you, Maddy. You've got it all wrong."

"Then what do you want?"

He ground his teeth as he tried to stop the first words which sprung from his own selfish needs to surface. But he had to think about her, now. "What do I want? I want you to go. That's what I want."

Her shocked eyes searched his face as if trying to find a dent, some flaw in the words she'd just heard. "What?" She pushed a strand of damp hair back from her face; her forehead scrunched into a frown. "What did you say?"

"I said, I want you to go. I want you to leave me, Belendroit, Akaroa, New Zealand if you want to. I want you to go far from here. I want you to go anywhere *but* here."

Her face creased into confusion. "But what about all you said about loving me? Was that all a lie?"

He couldn't answer her directly, all he could do was repeat himself. "It doesn't matter about any of that. There's only one thing I want from you now. And that's for you to leave here."

He sat back heavily and gritted his teeth, trying to stop himself from going back on his words—words which he meant with all his mind, but not all his heart.

He looked away as she rose and stood looking down at him.

"Gabe," she said softly. "Look at me and tell me to go."

He drew in a deep breath and rose, then stood before her and gripped her shoulders, staring her directly in the eyes. "You have to go, Maddy. You have to leave all this behind you and find your own path, not a path someone has arranged for you."

But the frown didn't leave her eyes. And for a moment he wondered if somewhere in the night she'd had a change of heart and had decided to stay. But it was too late now. There was no backing out of this. Besides, it didn't matter anyway, because he knew he was right. She had to leave because if she didn't, neither she, nor he, would ever know for sure whether she'd stayed for the right reasons—because she wanted to.

Jerkily he stepped back and dropped his arms to his side. He opened his mouth to speak, but what else could he say? So without waiting for a response, he pushed his hands into his pockets and strode back along the pier toward the town. His coat flapped in the wind, and the rain which had returned with renewed vigor soaked him instantly. But he couldn't have felt more chilled than he did already.

He didn't look back, he didn't need to. His final image of Maddy would be ingrained in his heart and mind forever: the wind whipping her hair around her face in which two eyes shone with tears.

He remembered the evening she'd first arrived at Belendroit when she'd sat stunned, surrounded by people who were busy talking and laughing. He'd been struck by that image at the time, wondering what it reminded him of. Now he knew. She was like a fly caught at the center of a massive spider's web—manipulated until she was well and truly placed where his family wanted her to be. And all he could do for her was to break the skeins of that web in which he, and Jonny and other Connelly family, had so firmly trapped her.

12

Three months later...

The palm trees which fringed the island tossed in the brisk wind blowing in from the Indian Ocean.

It had been three months since the day she'd flown out of New Zealand, told to leave by the man with whom she'd fallen in love. At the time she hadn't been able to see clearly. But now, three months later, she could. It had taken three months for her to understand.

She looked around the place which had been her refuge, where she'd managed to eke out her life on nothing but the inheritance that was solely hers now she'd turned twenty eight. Her uncle had once again come to her rescue by giving her the luxury of somewhere where she could lick her wounds, somewhere where she could allow her thoughts and feelings to settle, and where she could examine them and work out what had really happened.

It had only taken her two of the months to finally admit the truth, to see behind Gabe's actions. He was an honorable man, and trustworthy, and he'd done what he'd done because he knew that the final choice was up to her. If Jonny was the twin who'd loved her too intensely and wanted her held within his orbit even after his death, Gabe was the twin whose love had set her free. She'd felt so much for them both, but there was only one who she was able to love fully, without compromising herself, only one to whom she could commit forever.

It had taken her the third month to set her plans into action. She wanted to show Gabe that she trusted him, and what better way than to choose something freely, and commit to it totally, whether or not she ended up making a fool of herself—something she'd always tried to avoid. The fact that the date was exactly six months from the time she'd first arrived hadn't escaped her notice, and she knew it wouldn't escape Gabe's, but it was of no importance now.

She went up to the bar, and the bartender greeted her and passed her her usual soda water, as she sat down at the internet computer. She checked her emails and grinned as she read Amber's updates before turning to the Akaroa Facebook page to see what was going on. There was never any direct news from Gabe, but she could read between the lines of people talking about the different clubs, the hopes that people would recover from illnesses, the occasional death notice, knowing how it all impacted on Gabe. He simply carried on caring for people without making a big thing about it. It was central to who he was. And when he'd told her to leave, she'd thought he didn't want her anymore, when in fact it was the opposite. He was caring selflessly, yet again.

She looked out at the blue white-tipped waves, bright against the sky, and the white sandy beach. It felt like an age since she'd landed here, a confused and messed-up person. But time had unraveled her emotions and knots, and she could see more clearly now than she had at any other time of her life. Gabe had given her that. He'd given her space to reclaim herself, to work out what she felt, and where she wanted to be. He'd given her the space and freedom to decide for herself for once.

And she'd decided; she knew, now, what it was she wanted. But she couldn't walk back and claim it, because she had to prove to Gabe, after everything that had happened, that she could put her trust in another person, specifically Gabe. So how could she show him that she trusted him?

What had he accused her of? Hating to look a fool, not willing to trust, too passive in her acceptance of things. Well, she might have been once, but Gabe had given her the opportunity to change. What would be the biggest public statement she could make that would show him that she was no longer any of these things? That she could choose, of her own free will what it was she wanted, and what, or who, she trusted in? She could think of only one thing, and she couldn't do it from here.

She tipped the bartender but didn't tell him she wouldn't be back. She looked around for the last time and returned to the lodge to collect her bags. Her taxi would be arriving soon.

GABE WALKED along Beach Road in Akaroa, past the seat where he'd first met Maddy, and tried not to look at it. He succeeded, but it didn't help. He still felt her absence as keenly as if she'd been a part of him, prematurely lopped off, after his body had grown the nerve endings to support it. Like an amputated leg, his body still told him she was there. The trouble was, she wasn't. And he'd have to learn to live without her.

He continued down the street. It was only midday, but he'd finished work. Amber had asked him to take the afternoon off—something she'd never done before—so he had. He just hoped she didn't want to involve him in some hare-brained scheme involving her art, which he had no hope of appreciating, let alone understanding.

As always, when he was away from people, his thoughts turned to Maddy. Instead of lessening as time went by, he felt her absence more acutely. Was it always going to be like this? Instead of receding, his thoughts would swing back to her abruptly, like she'd shouted his name. Once the sound of Maddy calling his name had felt so real, he'd even gotten out of bed and looked outside, but the street had been empty. And he realized he was projecting his own feelings into his dreams. She was like a ghost who haunted him. He just hoped it wouldn't be forever, because a full night's sleep had become a distant memory.

Even now he thought he heard his name. Then he stopped and turned. He had. Amber was running down the street toward him, her red hair flying behind her, pink and orange dress a cloud of soft material, and a big smile in her perfectly oval face. He grinned back. Who wouldn't? You'd have to have a heart made of stone not to return Amber's smile.

"Amber! What are you doing here?"

"I know," she said breathlessly. "I'm usually in my studio at this time of the day, but I wanted to ask you something, and you weren't home."

He extracted his phone from his pocket. "Heard of one of these?"

She screwed up her face. "You know I don't carry one. All those wifi signals going through my body. You shouldn't either. You're a doctor, you should know."

"Okay, okay." He didn't want to get into another argument with his little sister about the dangers of modern technology. "What was it you wanted?"

She opened her mouth to answer but suddenly looked over Gabe's shoulder. Gabe followed Amber's wide-eyed stare to a man, tall, lean and fit, pounding the road with a confidence as if he owned it. As the man drew near—the picture of powerful athleticism—he and Amber exchanged a long hard look. It ignited a protective brotherly instinct in Gabe and he only just stopped himself from stepping between them. But then the man, whose expression hadn't changed apart from a hungry look in his eyes, had passed and he didn't look back. Unlike Amber, whose face was pink and eyes wide and glassy as she stared at his back.

"Who was that?" asked Amber.

Gabe shrugged as if it were normal to see a God running down the street, making cars stop for him on the narrow road. "How should I know? It's you who knows everyone around here."

Amber looked back at him as the subject of her inquiry turned a corner, without a backward glance. "Well, I've not seen him before, or heard of him."

"You've gone down in my estimation, Amber. I thought you knew everything about everyone around here."

"I have my informants, and they appear to have let me down." She tapped him on the chest. "Find out who he is for me, big brother. I wouldn't mind communing with nature with him." They fell into step. "He's tanned, so he likes to be outside. I bet he's a musician. He looks the part. Those eyes."

Gabe grunted. He hadn't liked what he'd seen in the man's eyes. They looked rapacious. Okay under normal circumstances, but not when trained on his little sister.

"Gabe, I mean it. I never see anyone I like, and now I have." She gave a pretend pout.

"You want me to go around asking after strange men?"

She turned to look. "He didn't look so strange."

"You know what I mean."

"Do it, won't you? For me. Ask around."

"Okay, okay. He's probably married with five kids."

"No. I'm sure he wasn't. He didn't look married."

"How do married people look?"

Amber shrugged. "It wasn't so much how he looked, it was the look he gave me. No married man would look at a woman that way."

Gabe opened his mouth to contradict her but sighed instead. There was no point. Whatever he said, Amber wouldn't believe him.

"So will you check him out for me?" she pressed.

"If that's what it takes to shut you up."

She grinned. No trace of pout remaining. Not that it ever did on Amber's face. "Yes, it is and thank you, sweetie. Now, let me return the favor and sort out your life for you."

"I'm off!" said Gabe doing an abrupt about turn. But Amber's soft grasp on his arm was enough to stop him. "Okay, what's up?"

"She wanted me to give this to you later, but if you're going to run off on me, I'd best give it to you now."

"What?"

She rummaged in her tasselled, hand-embroidered handbag, pulling out a string of beads, and glasses case, handing them to Gabe, so that she could delve more easily into her bag. "You don't even wear glasses!" he said, turning the round-rimmed glasses in his hand.

"No. But they're cute, and they were a bargain." She had a further rummage and pulled out an envelope, which looked as if it had been at the bottom of her bag for weeks. She held it out to him with a grin on her face.

"What the hell is this?" he asked, waving the envelope at her.

"Don't be so damn grumpy with me!" replied Amber. "Open it and see."

"You delivered it; you should know what it is."

She put her hands on her hips. "Maybe I do, and maybe I don't."

"What kind of answer is that?" asked Gabe, slitting the envelope and extracting a single sheet of paper with only a few paragraphs handwritten on it.

"The only answer you're likely to get."

"Who the hell sends letters through the mail—" He stopped as he scanned its contents. "Oh." He exhaled the word and turned away from Amber, not wanting her to be a witness to his reaction. He couldn't have spoken anyway, all the breath was knocked out of him.

An invitation from Maddy to meet him at Christchurch airport. She was arriving that afternoon. And he'd canceled all his appointments because his sister had requested him to.

He swung around and waved the paper. "You knew about this, didn't you?"

Amber raised her eyebrows and failed to control a grin. "Yes. You don't mind, do you? She wanted to make sure you'd be able to come. She wanted my help."

He nodded, a thousand thoughts and feelings fighting for attention in his brain, but only one surfaced. Maddy wanted to meet him. Before he could force himself to be reasonable, hope triumphed. She wanted to see *him*. His heart thudded, and he felt alive for the first time since she'd left. He allowed a vision of her face to fill his mind, something he'd been continually repressing since she'd left. Her hair flowing around her face, the way she shyly pushed it behind her ear as she looked at him. And then he thought of her eyes, cautious, distrustful. And his heart sank again. Maybe she was here to see the others, to check out the archaeological dig she'd worked on, and was only meeting with him first to get it over with. She may be distrustful, but she'd wasn't cruel. No, this was a social call only. He felt slightly sick as the adrenaline ebbed away as fast as it had come.

"Amber, tell me, why has she come back?"

"I think she had some unfinished business here," she said, with a twisted smile, as if trying to prevent herself from saying something.

"Amber," he said warningly. "You know something, and you're not telling me. Is it something connected to the dig?"

She shrugged. "I can't say."

"Can't, or won't."

"The difference doesn't matter. I'm *not* saying. Now, why don't you stop asking me stupid questions and get in your car and go to the airport and ask her yourself."

"Great, an hour's drive to be told to get lost."

"Maybe she'd like to see you. Have you thought of that?"

"To return something? To tell me to go to hell?"

"Now, why would she come all the way back to New Zealand to tell you to go to hell?"

"I don't know! I don't know anything anymore. Particularly when it comes to women."

Amber put her arm around him and rested her cheek on his arm. He shook his head.

"It's okay, Gabe. Just give her a chance."

"Do you know anything, Amber? Please, if you know what it is she wants, put me out of my misery."

She lifted her cheek and looked up at him. "There's nothing to worry about. This is Maddy, remember. She wouldn't hurt you."

"Amber, she already has."

Sadness flooded Amber's face, and Gabe immediately regretted his words.

"You will go, won't you?" she asked plaintively.

"Of course I'll go. God knows why. But you know I love her. I'd go to the ends of the earth if she asked me to."

"Lucky for you it's only to Christchurch." She grinned. He wished he shared Amber's confidence.

MADDY'S FLIGHT from Thailand had been delayed, and she was a bundle of nerves as she walked into the arrivals hall. She didn't need to go to baggage claims, she had all she needed on her. She glanced at the clock. She had half-an-hour before she met Gabe. She looked around and found a seat in the corner opposite the entrance. She checked the time again. She just had time to get a coffee. Jetlag was already making her feel dizzy.

Maddy had to wait in the queue which took forever because the coffee machine was faulty. But an anxious glance at the clock revealed she still had time. Finally, coffee in hand, she turned around and bumped into someone and spilled coffee down his shirt.

"I'm so sorry!"

The coffee stain was spreading fast. He pulled his shirt away from his body. "That's hot! Good to see you too, Maddy!"

She looked up into blue eyes, full of humor.

"Gabe!" It wasn't so much his name as a shout from her soul; a name that had filled her heart and mind for so long that it rushed out on the edge of her breath. She was frozen to the spot, unable to take her eyes from his.

It was Gabe who made the first move. He reached out and took her coffee from her shaking hand with a cautious smile. "How about I take it. It might save both our clothes."

She nodded and swallowed. "I'm so sorry."

He looked uncertain as if he wasn't sure what she was apologizing for. But he obviously decided that, whatever it was, she was forgiven. "No problem."

"Thank you," she breathed weakly.

"Shall we take a seat?"

"Yes, sure. Sorry." Maddy bit her lip. She wondered if she'd ever be able to stop apologizing to Gabe.

She followed him to the seating area, trying desperately to regain any sense of equilibrium she may have had at the start of the journey. But then he turned and looked at her, a curious mix of wariness and affection in his eyes, and she wondered if she was a million miles off target. Whether her interpretation of events here had been skewed by all those months on a Thai beach. That he didn't feel the way she imagined he'd felt for her. But it was too late to turn back.

He placed the coffee gingerly on the table and wiped his hands on the napkin which surrounded it. He sat down, leaned forward, his forearms on his knees and looked up at her with eyes that suggested he had far more control over the situation than she had.

"Well?" he coaxed.

"Yes, fine thanks."

His grin broadened. "As happy as I am that you're feeling well, it was the kind of 'well' which is meant to prompt a disclosure. *Well*"—he opened his hands in a sweeping gesture —"as in, 'and so, why am I here?'"

"Right. Sorry." A wave of heat prickled her skin. She'd never felt such a fool, but she had to continue. She dragged in a shaky breath, but it did nothing to calm her. "I asked you to come because I have a question for you."

He waited for her to continue but, with her suddenly dry mouth, what she had to say stayed in her head. "Go on," he coaxed. "Tell me the worst."

He imagined the worst! That loosened her tongue. Except all the words she'd rehearsed went out of her mind, instead her feelings diverted her to the moment he'd made her see herself for who she had been—not an independent, decisive woman, but a scared one.

"Do you remember that time when we were swimming with the dolphins?"

His eyebrows raised and he sat back with a laugh. "Of course. I'll never forget it. Is that why you asked me here? To challenge my memories of our times together?"

She shrugged and frowned. "In a way, yes. You see, it was the first time in a long time that I didn't worry about what people thought of me, about how I was perceived—I was so present, in that moment of time, that that mask, that barrier I'd placed between me and the world, fell right away." She looked at him. "And you noticed."

"Yes, I noticed. I remember it well. I felt I'd seen you properly for the first time."

She smiled and grunted. "And you told me that everyone should risk everything for what they felt in their heart." She shrugged, feeling awkward.

"'Everyone', 'they'—I meant you of course."

"Yeah, I know. And I told you that I didn't know what I felt in my heart." She looked up, and all awkwardness vanished. "But that was then. I know now." She fisted her hand and held it against her chest, urging him, wanting him to understand exactly what she felt there. "I want to lay everything on the line for what I feel, here, inside."

"Everything?"

"Yes. I've always hated showing my feelings to the world in case they got trampled on. A case of self-preservation, I guess. But I don't need that any longer. I'm stronger than I've ever been, and that's down to you. You've healed me."

He grunted softly and sat back. "That's what I do; I'm a doctor after all."

She shook her head vigorously. "No, I don't mean that. I'm sorry, I'm not explaining myself well at all. What I mean"—she took another deep breath—"is that, because of you, I can see more clearly now. *Feel* more clearly."

"Well, that's good. So where to from here?"

"To Belendroit."

"To Belendroit?" he asked.

She licked her lips again. "Yes. I've some unfinished business there."

"Right," he nodded, the question answered. "Right," he repeated. It might have been answered, but she could see it wasn't the answer he'd hoped for. "I guess you want to see my family?"

"Of course," she said, the real reason on the tip of her tongue, but she refused to reveal it yet. She had something to prove first.

"Something to do with the fact that it's six months to the day when you first came?"

She nodded, not trusting herself to spill the real reason she wanted to go to Belendroit.

"Right. Let's go and get this over with."

Her heart contracted, but she couldn't weaken. She'd done enough of that over the past year. She needed to show Gabe that she knew what she wanted now.

GABE LIFTED his focus from the road briefly to glance at Maddy, who had remained strangely quiet for most of the journey to Belendroit. He hadn't a clue what she was up to, and he wasn't going to pry. It was up to her now. Instead, he focused on the winding road, refusing to acknowledge the turmoil of feelings which having Maddy seated at his side brought forth. He pushed them down, just as he did when he was working for *Médecins Sans Frontières* when there was a rush on the field hospital after a violent clash, and guts spilled from wounds, parts of bodies were missing, and the stench and terror of death filled the air. At times like those he could literally feel his head cooling, his eyes and senses slowing, assessing, prioritizing, dealing with the mayhem while others around him either froze or panicked. He'd always had that ability. And it kicked in now. Except there were no wounded, only Maddy who appeared the least wounded he'd ever seen her.

"The leaves," said Maddy. "They're nearly gone." She turned to Gabe with a wistful half-smile.

"Ah, you'll find that's what happens when it's nearly winter," said Gabe, refusing to heed the kick in his gut that her tentative smile gave him.

Maddy flashed him a grin at his attempt at humor. "Somehow in my mind, it had remained the same."

"Nothing remains the same," he said, shifting gears as they turned into a tight bend. The car revved up a steep incline, clinging to the edge of a cliff which rose above the harbor, a streak of sapphire amid emerald green hills.

Maddy caught her breath. "It's such a contrast to where I've been."

Gabe gave Maddy time to elaborate as he smoothly settled the car into top gear as they hit a straight piece of road. She didn't. "Are you going to tell me where you've been?"

She raised an eyebrow and smiled. "If you ask."

"Consider yourself asked."

"Yes. I've been in Thailand, on the island of Ko Samet."

"And what were you doing there for so long?" For some reason, a flash of jealousy zapped through him. A beautiful woman like Maddy in a well-known tourist resort. She would have been the object of many men's desires. "Having fun?"

The smile turned into a frown. "I wouldn't describe it as fun."

"Come on; Ko Samet is party central."

"Not where I was. I stayed in a small resort on the other

side of the island. It was very quiet, peaceful. It gave me time and space to think about things."

"And your thoughts led you to returning here. Almost six months to the day, just as Jonny wanted you to?"

She nodded.

Gabe's gut tightened with nausea. He slammed on the brakes a little too hard to slow down for a corner. He was aware of Maddy lurching forward slightly in response. This was ridiculous. Was all this some kind of joke? He loved her, whether she knew that or not. He wasn't about to tell her again. What was the point? She simply wanted to complete her promise to Jonny and to catch up with the rest of his family to say the goodbye which she'd omitted to do when she left three months earlier.

They entered the town of Akaroa and wound around the harbor toward Belendroit. Gabe waved to a couple of people before they came out the other side of the town. The sun was slow to burn off the mist and, despite the fact it was mid-afternoon, the light was hazy, and Belendroit appeared almost ethereal amidst its surrounding trees.

"I don't know if anyone is home, but I guess your visit is more symbolic than anything. I guess it doesn't matter to you if anyone is there or not."

"That's a lot of guesses," she said lightly.

He shrugged. "It's all I have."

She grunted as if hurt and looked away. He was immediately sorry. He wouldn't hurt her for the world, even if she didn't love him.

He turned into the driveway and was surprised to see some cars parked. "Strange," he said peering out the front window across the cars. "Looks like some of the family are here." He looked at her. "Anything to do with you?"

She shot him a quick, nervous smile. "Yes."

He watched her as she got out the car and looked around.

She was up to something, and whatever it was, she was determined to keep him in the dark. And all he could do was follow, and find out what was going on. It was an unusual feeling for him, for someone else to be in control and him following. And there was only one person in the world who could do it without him resisting—Maddy.

He followed her past the barking cocker spaniels—Stanley and Boo were quite ecstatic to see her—and on, toward the house. Strangely there was no one on the veranda, and, even stranger, it was tidy. There wasn't a teapot or roughly folded newspaper in sight.

Gabe shot Maddy a suspicious look but before he could ask her anything she'd run up the steps and disappeared into the house, just as his father emerged from around the corner of the house.

"Gabe!"

"Dad," Gabe greeted. "What's going on?" He began to follow Maddy, but his father reached out and put his arm around him and gave him a big hug. His father had always been emotionally demonstrative, but something didn't feel right. Maybe it was the way his father retained a firm grip on his shoulder.

"Going on? Why would you ask that? Can't a father hug his son?"

Gabe narrowed his eyes, never leaving his father's, who looked positively mischievous.

"*Something*," said Gabe with emphasis, "is going on. And I'd like to know what."

His father grinned. "That's the lot of us men, son. Women always know what's going on, and we find out eventually, but only when they're ready to tell us."

Gabe opened his mouth to respond, but his father interrupted, after looking over Gabe's shoulder.

"It was the same with your mother, you know. She knew

best, always did. Not that I ever realized that until after the event." He sighed heavily. "Anyway, I digress. Did you know that we received a standing ovation at the last showing of our play at the repertory?"

Gabe shook his head. "Yes, Dad. I know, I was there. Well done." Again, his father gave a quick glance over Gabe's shoulder. This time he smiled and Gabe was able to take his father's hand from his shoulder without undue force. Just a last clap on the back. "What on earth is going on. Have you all gone mad?" He turned to see Maddy standing in the porch dressed in a long white bridal gown. Amber's hand reached out from the hallway and handed her a posy of flowers, and quickly brushed away a crease in the dress, before disappearing, leaving Maddy alone.

"You're getting married?" he asked, hardly able to breathe.

"I hope so."

He swallowed. "Who to?"

"To you, if you'll have me." She sucked in a deep breath. "Gabriel Connelly, will you marry me?"

Gabe looked around, wondering if this was a trick, but his father had also disappeared. There were just the two of them on the family veranda, whose furnishings were eclipsed by the russet and golds of the misty autumnal afternoon.

"Really, Maddy? You bring me here, six months to the day that Jonny asked you to stay here and ask me to marry you? You're doing exactly what Jonny wanted you to do. You're doing this for him, aren't you?"

"No, please believe me I'm not. I needed those months to be on my own and to think about things. You gave me that space, and I've used it."

"And at the end of that time, you return and say you want to marry me. Again, Maddy, I ask you, why?"

Her smile dropped. "Because… because I love you." Her voice was hoarse. "You asked me how I felt before I went away, and I was feeling too crazy to answer you properly. But now I can. I was scared to have feelings, but you gave me the time to heal, to think things through." She threw her arms up helplessly. "Time to miss you so much that I knew I couldn't live without you. Gabe, I love you. Will you marry me?"

He shook his head and took the bouquet from her, smoothing his thumbs over the back of her hands. "And I love you. Nothing has changed there. But how can I be sure you're not simply doing what you think I want, what Jonny wanted?"

"I knew you'd say that. I knew that you were just as lacking in trust as I was. So I'm going to do something that will prove to you I've changed. I want to show you exactly how far I've come, show you that I'm no longer afraid to stake a claim on life, on someone's heart."

He smiled. "And how do you intend to do that?"

"I've lived my life in the shadows too long. Pretending I'm not there so I won't be noticed, moving to someone else's plan."

"You're going to step out of the shadows." He stroked her hair. "Darling, I hate to tell you this, but you've been walking in brilliant sunlight ever since I saw you. You might see yourself in the shadows, but no one else does."

"Then it's time I became the woman who I appear to be, the woman I was destined to be."

"Good," he said softly. "And how do you propose to do this?"

"I've asked you twice now if you'll marry me and you haven't given me a proper answer. I'm going to ask you one more time, but not here, not in the shadows of the veranda."

"Where then?"

"Come with me." She tugged his hand and followed her down the steps and around the side of the house, to the rear, which looked out across a narrow stretch of grass down to the beach and out onto the water.

The first thing he saw was Aimee, his niece, crouching over a daisy chain, her white dress bunched around her knees. "Hey Aimee? What are you doing here?"

Aimee jumped up and ran squealing out of sight. He followed Maddy down the path until they emerged onto the sunlit back lawn where one by one his family revealed themselves to him. They stood around an arch which was covered in flowers.

For once Gabe was at a loss for words. No one said anything, just grinned stupidly at him. His father stood beside Max whose smug expression could only be read as "it's your turn now, bro". Lizzi and Pete stood close, holding hands, watching Gabe with barely suppressed grins. Rachel and Zane—his best mate—stood openly grinning, obviously enjoying Gabe's discomfort, and Amber was there also. Except Amber's eyes were shadowed and were looking at Maddy. It made Gabe turn to Maddy who'd walked over to the arch and stood waiting for him.

Gabe smiled at everyone and walked up to Maddy. She cleared her throat, but he reached out and took both her hands in his.

"Maddy!"

"I want to ask you—"

"No! Stop right there."

There was a collective intake of breath from everyone, and Amber gave an unconcealed squeal of horror.

"I don't want you to ask me anything, Maddy, I really don't."

She looked stunned, but Gabe pressed on, knowing with all his heart that this was the only course of action he wanted now. Her mouth opened and a barely audible "why?" emerged.

"Because"—he dropped down to one knee—"I want to ask you if you'll do me the honor of becoming my wife."

It took several seconds for everyone to comprehend that the tables had been turned.

He could see a myriad of feelings and thoughts flit across her face, usually closed to everyone, but not to him, not now. The pain of rejection had been replaced by a look of delight, quickly followed by disbelief. Instinctively he rose and took her in his arms. "I want you to marry me, Maddy. I've never loved anyone as I have you, and I never will. I want to be by your side for the rest of my life. Will you have me?"

The tears trickled from her eyes before she nodded and a strangled sound emerged.

He grinned. "Is that a yes?"

"Yes!"

He kissed her briefly and then looked around for his father. "Dad? I take it you're going to do the honors here?"

"Certainly am, son. I wouldn't let anyone else marry you two."

His family jostled around, congratulating them before settling back into a group as his father took center stage beneath the arch with them, and began to read out the words of the marriage ceremony.

As Gabe listened to the vows which Maddy had written, he heard her expression of love, and he heard the words of his brother Jonny. It was almost as if Jonny was there as Maddy's closest relative, giving her away in marriage, just as he'd intended when he believed that he wouldn't survive to be with her.

"And will you, Gabriel Connelly, take Madeleine MacGillivray to be your lawfully wedded wife. Yours to cherish, in sickness and in health, for as long as you shall both live."

"Yes. I'll cherish her always."

. . .

As Maddy's new family surrounded her, hugging and kissing her, congratulating her, and laughing at the last-minute turn of events, she felt cherished, like she never had before, in the arms of the man she adored, surrounded by a family who she knew would always be there for her. It was Jonny's final gift to her—a marriage not made in heaven, but here on earth, between two people who loved each other more than life itself.

EPILOGUE

Gabe took a swig of beer but didn't take his eyes off the astrolabe which took pride of place above the dresser, surrounded by family photographs and other treasures. His gaze rested on the inscription which he'd seen many times since he'd retrieved the object from the sand, but whose meaning he hadn't known until today. It felt like the final link, a final settling in his heart.

Suddenly, the door suddenly burst open and Maddy entered the house on a rush of cold air. She shivered loudly as she unpeeled her scarf and shrugged off her coat and hooked them on the coat stand.

"Man, it's cold out there!"

"Cold? I thought you Scandinavians were used to the cold!" Gabe teased, rising to greet her. She laughed, more easily now than she used to, and kissed him, her cold nose brushing his warm cheek and rousing his desire for her. He wondered if it would ever diminish; he doubted it.

"Denmark seems a lifetime away."

"A lifetime? Where's my scientific wife gone? It's been

fifteen months to be exact since you arrived in New Zealand."

"Fifteen months? Is that all? Shows it doesn't take long to feel at home."

He loved it when she said things like that. He caressed her swelling stomach, and kissed her again. "So have you been at the new dig?"

"Yes. There's a lot to do, but it looks promising."

He frowned. "You shouldn't be working so hard now you're pregnant."

"Come on, you know I'm careful. Besides, since when has a doctor told a perfectly fit woman to stop work?"

"Since that woman is his wife."

"Gabe," she said in a warning tone.

"Madeleine," he said in the same tone. He pushed away a strand of her hair from her cheek. "You know I'll always support you in everything you do, but I also made a vow which I intend to keep—to cherish and care for you."

He was rewarded with a look of love. "I know. And I love that. But there's no need to worry." Her hand strayed to the swollen curves of her stomach. "I can look after myself." She glanced toward the kitchen and sniffed appreciatively. "Talking of which…" Maddy might have opened up emotionally over the past year, but some things didn't change—she still loved her food. He sat down again so he could see her better. "Anyway, I wasn't working," she continued.

Gabe grunted in surprise. Maddy grinned at him, but didn't elaborate. He refused to ask where she'd been—that smacked of a possessive husband and while he might cherish her totally, he had no desire to try to control her.

"Something smells good!" she said, pulling off her cardigan as she went. She peered into the oven. "You've made dinner. Not only smells good, but looks good, too!"

"Yes, well, I know which sister to go to for specific skills —Rachel for cooking, and Amber, *not* for cooking."

"Amber's art skills are in hot demand and it doesn't look like her new man is concerned about her lack of culinary prowess."

"True." Gabe frowned. He hadn't yet made up his mind about Amber's new man. He wasn't like anyone in the family, and certainly nothing like any of Amber's previous boyfriends.

His musings were interrupted by Maddy's arm snaking around his shoulders as she sat on his lap. She wriggled a little and he groaned. "Just as well you're my wife, Ms Madeleine," he said pushing her hair back from her cold cheek, "otherwise what I'm about to propose would be considered indecent."

She raised an eyebrow and wriggled on his lap again. "Aren't you going to ask me where I've been?"

"No." He wasn't going to admit that where she'd been was the last thing on his mind. He tried his best to re-focus. "But you're welcome to tell me if you like."

She pouted, and he grinned. She never used to pout. And he'd spent many happy hours exploring that pout. He reined in his focus once more.

"Next door," she said.

He raised his eyebrows in surprise. "Which next door?"

"Mrs. King. I took her some groceries. She's not feeling so well since her family returned home."

"Mrs. King is taking advantage of you."

"Is that right?" she asked, bringing her body, still cold from the chill winter air, tight against his warm one. It was all he could do to concentrate on what he was saying.

"Yes. There's nothing wrong with Mrs. King. I saw her a few days ago."

Maddy cocked her head to one side. "I know she's okay

physically. But she's lonely. And I know all about lonely, now that I'm not."

His heart melted all over again. He swallowed and grunted something which might have been 'well,' or might have been 'okay'. Whatever word his grunt formed, Maddy understood and kissed him again.

"So how's *your* day been?" she asked.

"Busy. I worked late tonight."

She inspected his face and brushed her finger under his eyes. "You're looking tired. It's you who works too hard, not me."

And he knew it. Since Jonny had died he'd felt he had to live his life for two people—for him and Jonny. But maybe no longer. He glanced at the astrolabe once more. Maddy shifted and followed his gaze.

"It's not been all work and no play," said Gabe. "Ben called round earlier."

"Ben from the university?"

"Yes, that Ben. I think he was hoping to talk with you about the dig, but we had a beer and he saw the astrolabe." Gabe was watching her carefully. "And he translated the inscription on it." He turned Maddy's face to his. "You didn't know, did you?"

"What?" She glanced away, and he couldn't see her face. "About the inscription? I know it's there, but I can't remember the exact translation. Ancient languages aren't my specialty." She shook her head and turned back to him with a smile. "Fancy a cup of tea?" She stood up and filled the kettle.

"No, thanks." He unhooked the astrolabe from the wall and traced his finger over the engraved brass, mentally reciting the words which Ben had told him. "So you *did* know the translation at one time, then?"

She hesitated before switching on the kettle. "Yes." She turned to him, leaned against the kitchen bench, and folded her arms. "Yes," she repeated. "Jonny knew it. He loved poetry and apparently the inscription was a quotation from some Persian poet."

"Rumi," he said.

She nodded and smiled. "Rumi! That's right." She came and took the astrolabe from Gabe. "Did Ben translate it for you?"

Gabe swallowed and nodded. "He took a photo, and he's going to send me a full translation."

"Cool. That'll be interesting. I can't really remember the translation which Jonny told me. It seems a long time ago."

Gabe smiled briefly as the final line which Ben had translated for him echoed around his head once more, as it had been all evening. He'd tell her later, but not now. She'd moved on, just as he and Jonny had wanted her to do.

He turned to see Maddy linger, looking at the astrolabe as she re-hung it on the wall. She traced the inscription lightly with her finger. A shadow of a sad smile settled briefly on her face before she turned and left the room. He wondered whether she knew more than she was letting on. Somehow he didn't think he'd ever know, didn't think he'd ever completely lift the veil of mystery from Maddy. And somehow he knew he didn't want to.

He turned his attention back to the astrolabe whose Persian characters were muted in the antique brass, worn away by human hands and the elements, but still decipherable. Especially the final sentence which had been protected by the raised edge. He whispered the words softly to himself.

There are a thousand ways to go home again.

And Jonny had found a way—a way for them all.

AFTERWORD

Thank you for reading *Yours to Cherish,* book 3 in the Lantern Bay series. I hope you enjoyed it! Reviews are always welcome—they help me, and they help prospective readers to decide if they'd enjoy the book.

Other books in the Lantern Bay series are:

Yours to Give
Yours to Treasure
Yours to Cherish
Yours to Keep

The next book in the series—Yours to Keep—features Amber and her mystery jogger. An excerpt follows.

You can check out all my books on the following pages. And, if you'd like to know when my next book is available, you can sign up for my new release e-mail list via my website —dianafraser.com.

Happy reading!

Diana

YOURS TO KEEP

BOOK 4 OF LANTERN BAY—AMBER

Excerpt

Amber Connelly looked up as the cafe bell clanged. She

didn't do it every time—that would have been plain crazy as the cafe was a busy place—no, only at five minutes past one every day, excepting weekends. She watched the tall, broad-shouldered man in the business suit—the only suited person in the cafe—walk past her without looking at her and take a seat by the window. He picked up a menu and studied it. Why, she didn't know. He must have known exactly its contents by now. And, besides, he always chose the same thing.

She was just collecting her pen and paper when the door opened again and Gabe and Maddy entered, laughing and holding hands. She grinned to see her brother and sister-in-law so happy. The suited man raised an eyebrow at the noise, as if irritated by the distraction, before returning to peruse the menu. As Gabe walked by he caught the eye of the man and Amber could sense a bristling. Gabe, being protective as usual.

Amber waved them to their usual table and walked up to the man. He was aware of her presence, she knew that even though he didn't look up immediately. She smiled to herself. He really did intrigue her, even though he wasn't anything like the type of guy she was usually interested in.

She smiled. "Good morning. How are you today?"

He looked up and, as usual, her heart nearly stopped. Surely it was indecent for a man to be endowed with such beautiful green eyes. "It's afternoon," he said.

"Oh! So it is," she said unable to focus on anything but those eyes.

"It's past twelve, which is the middle of the day, so it's afternoon. You were incorrect," he added for good measure, as if she doubted his words. She didn't. She only ever doubted herself. Everyone else—especially this man who she imagined would be incapable of error—she always accepted as being correct.

She grinned, and his eyes narrowed.

She chuckled at his response and he frowned.

She laughed out loud—really, he must be the straightest, most pedantic man she'd ever met—and he looked away, back at the menu, his frown deepening. She felt the brightness fade from the day as he turned his eyes away. She wanted to see them looking at her again.

"You're right! Of course it's afternoon. I should know, we're serving lunch." She ducked her head so he couldn't hide from her gaze. "So what's it to be?"

She was rewarded with another look from those green eyes, their composure once more intact. He handed her the menu. "Cesar salad with chicken. Keep the dressing to one side. Are the wholemeal rolls fresh?"

"Fresh?" Amber repeated the last word he'd said, hoping it would help her concentrate on what he was saying.

"Yes. The rolls. Are they fresh? I only want them if they've been freshly made today."

Jeez, he was one out the box, this guy. "Everything's fresh. The rolls were baked this morning with my own fair hands."

Those green eyes slid down to her hands and she suddenly felt self-conscious about the ring she was wearing. She wasn't supposed to wear rings but must have forgotten to slip off the large greenstone and silver ring she'd inherited from her mother.

"When I said 'fair' hands," she began to blather, trying to slide the ring around and hide her hands under the notebook on which she was taking his order. "I meant you know, reliable hands. Because they're not that fair. Not really."

"In what way are they 'not fair'? They look perfectly fair to me. Well formed, and..." he hesitated, uncharacteristically, "quite attractive actually."

"Oh!" The single word slid out as if she'd been punched. She wasn't smiling any longer. Instead she felt that curious sensation in her stomach she experienced whenever she saw him, step up a notch. "Thank you." She held up her hand. "Yes, I suppose they're not bad, are they?"

"No. So if you agree, what did you mean when you said they're not fair?"

"Oh, that." She shrugged and wrinkled her nose self-deprecatingly. "I just mean that I'm not that good a cook. Enthusiastic but, from all accounts—well by my family's accounts—not actually that good."

"And yet you've made the bread rolls. You're not doing a good job at selling them to me."

"I'm good at rolls. Anything with yeast is okay because I can give it a bit of a bash. Heavy handed you see?" she said, slamming her hand on the table. Everyone looked around but the man himself didn't move an inch. Instead he touched her ring, accidentally brushing the back of her hand as he did so.

"Heavy hands maybe." He looked back into eyes that had dropped the facade and made her melt deep inside. "But they're beautiful ones."

She took an involuntary step back, wondering if she'd heard right. This was the rude guy, right? Not someone who flattered. She didn't reply and turned abruptly.

"Excuse me!" he called after her. She stopped in her tracks, and turned slowly, wondering what on earth he was going to say. Was he about to tell her that he was wrong, her hands weren't in the slightest bit beautiful, or maybe that he didn't want his lunch after all? Maybe she'd dreamed the whole thing.

"Yes?" She asked breathlessly.

"And a coffee please. Short black."

"Right," she said, more to herself than to him. "Right. Coffee it is." Coffee it was every day. If there was one thing that the green-eyed man who made her legs go weak was,

was predictable. But, as she walked over to her brother's table, she considered the word. Predictable was a bit negative. Maybe regular, or 'knows what he wants'. Yes, that was infinitely better. Because he'd just turned out to be anything but predictable.

ALSO BY DIANA FRASER

The Mackenzies

The Real Thing

The PA's Revenge

The Marriage Trap

The Cowboy's Craving

The Playboy's Redemption

The Lakehouse Café

Lantern Bay

Yours to Give

Yours to Treasure

Yours to Cherish

Yours to Keep

Desert Kings

Wanted: A Wife for the Sheikh

The Sheikh's Bargain Bride

The Sheikh's Lost Lover

Awakened by the Sheikh

Claimed by the Sheikh

Wanted: A Baby by the Sheikh

The Sheikhs of Havilah

The Sheikh's Secret Baby

Bought by the Sheikh

The Sheikh's Forbidden Lover

Italian Romance

Perfect

Her Retreat

Trusting Him

An Accidental Christmas

Printed in Great Britain
by Amazon

51120812R00129